"I can't sta
Dean said

He was already halfway down the stairs, but Laura could still see the remorse in those scaldingly blue eyes. "Why?" she asked.

His eyes closed briefly. When they opened, they held a look of grim resolve that made her shiver.

He stalked up the stairs two at a time, his gaze locked on her.

She backed up into her room until she felt the foot of her bed against her legs.

He dropped his duffel and uniform on the landing, crossed to her in three long strides, wrapped his hands around her head and kissed her.

On the mouth this time, and hard. His mouth plundered hers, took it savagely, hungrily. It shocked her, made her heart hammer wildly, every nerve in her body tighten with alarm....

And need.

He released her and backed away, his chest pumping, his eyes mirroring the fierce panic rioting through her.

"Okay?" he rasped. "Now do you see why I have to go?"

Dear Reader,

Back when Regis Philbin's millionaire game show
was just a twinkle in some television producer's eye,
I started toying with the idea of using a million-dollar
windfall as the vehicle for a romance. To the very rich,
a million dollars is pocket change. But to most of us,
it's still...well, a million dollars, with the power to
change our lives. Maybe even with the power to bring
together two people with only one thing in common:
a simmering passion for each other that they've both
kept deeply buried...except for one explosive night six
years ago, a night that has haunted their waking hours
and fueled their restless dreams ever since.

Now for the characters. One of my favorites is the
untamable bad-boy hero, the lone wolf. And who
better to team him up with than a down-to-earth
woman for whom marriage and motherhood are
everything.

Million Dollar Baby is the story that developed
when I threw these two people together with a million
dollars. I'd love to hear what you think of it. You can
e-mail me at my Web site, which is linked to the
Harlequin site www.eHarlequin.com.

Enjoy!

Patricia Ryan

Books by Patricia Ryan

HARLEQUIN TEMPTATION
602—FOR THE THRILL OF IT
631—TWICE THE SPICE
696—SUMMER HEAT
701—IN HOT PURSUIT
764—ALL OF ME

MILLION DOLLAR BABY
Patricia Ryan

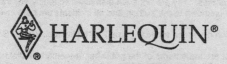

HARLEQUIN®

TORONTO • NEW YORK • LONDON
AMSTERDAM • PARIS • SYDNEY • HAMBURG
STOCKHOLM • ATHENS • TOKYO • MILAN • MADRID
PRAGUE • WARSAW • BUDAPEST • AUCKLAND

To Doranna Durgin, fellow novelist, friend and gearhead
extraordinaire. What a long, strange trip it's been.

Many thanks to Antoinette Stockenberg, who cheerfully allowed me
to ransack her brain for information about sailboats and
wintering aboard. Her help was invaluable to this landlubber.
Thanks also to the divine Susan Sheppard for filling in the
remaining blanks. If, after all their help, there are still some
sailing bloopers, the fault is entirely mine.

ISBN 0-373-25906-9

MILLION DOLLAR BABY

Copyright © 2000 by Patricia Ryan.

This edition published by arrangement with Harlequin Books S.A.

® and TM are trademarks of the publisher. Trademarks indicated with
® are registered in the United States Patent and Trademark Office, the
Canadian Trade Marks Office and in other countries.

Visit us at www.eHarlequin.com

Printed In U.S.A.

1

DAMN, NOT ANOTHER reporter.

The man walking purposefully toward Dean Kettering on the pier was one of those bulky, aging, Irish ward boss types with a thatch of snowy hair and a candy-apple-red nose, his trench coat flapping open over a suit and loosened tie.

Facing away from him, Dean untied the last of the lines securing the canvas tarp that shielded the *Lorelei* from snow and ice. A wooden boat needed to breathe, so Dean liked to take advantage of sunny mornings like this to give her a little air—even if it *was* colder than hell. Winter was dragging on pretty late this year all over the Northeast, but its claws had sunk particularly deep in New England, pummeled over the past couple of weeks by a barrage of March snowstorms.

"Mr. Kettering?" the man called in a deep-chested wheeze.

Muttering a curse under his breath, Dean leaped onto the thirty-six-foot sloop and started hauling up the weighty canvas. He had neither the time nor inclination to play hero du jour on the ten o'clock news. You'd think the local press would have figured that out by now.

"Mr. Kettering?" The stranger's shoes crunched

heavily on the ice-crusted pier. "'Scuse me. You are Dean Kettering, aren't you?"

Dean twisted his wind-whipped hair and shoved it under the turtleneck collar of the oversize Shetland sweater that he wore over two sweatshirts. Adjusting his fingerless gloves, he started dragging the tarp over the *Lorelei*'s well-varnished teak deck.

"This is you, right?" Dean's unwanted visitor held up a copy of the *Providence Journal*—the March 19 edition, Dean saw, because he recognized yesterday's front-page article headlined Portsmouth's Publicity-Shy Hero.

The article was accompanied by two pictures of Dean. The first was a posed portrait of him neatly shorn and in the Air Force uniform he hadn't worn in four years. The second, snapped yesterday during the press onslaught, showed him turning away from the camera, his face half obscured by his overgrown hair, holding a hand up to ward off the photographer.

Hauling up the tarp, Dean said, "You're wasting your time, pal. Take your little steno pad and go home."

"I don't have a steno pad."

"Your tape recorder, then."

"Listen, *pal*, I don't know who you think I am, but my name is George Walsh, and I'm here to give you—"

"Go away."

"Are you always such a pain in the ass to strangers?"

"Only when I want them to go away."

"And you're not in the least bit curious as to why I'm here?"

"I know why you're here." Dean grunted as he yanked the tarp back. "You want to ram those fifteen minutes of fame down my throat whether I like it or not—only I'm not playing that game."

"You've got it all—"

"The interview is over." Dean turned his back on Walsh as he worked.

"I didn't come here to interview you, Kettering."

"Look, don't try and pull one over on me, okay? Whatever it is you think you're gonna finesse me into—"

"I came here to give you a million dollars."

Dean paused and gave an incredulous little shake of his head. "Go away."

"Did you hear what I said?"

Dean turned, hands on hips, to face Walsh. "Listen, I told you—"

"Here it is." Walsh unzipped his bulging Lands' End briefcase, withdrew a green envelope and held it out to him.

"What's that?"

"A check for a million dollars."

"Uh-huh. Right." Dean continued gathering up the tarp.

Walsh rolled his eyes. "Just look at it, for cryin' out loud. It's a cashier's check for a million dollars made out in your name."

"Go. Away."

"I don't think you understand. I really and truly am giving you a million dollars here. Tax free."

"And what do I have to do to earn it? Get interviewed on national television and kiss my privacy goodbye forever?" Having uncovered the *Lorelei*'s deck, Dean stood and rotated his shoulders.

"I'm no reporter, Kettering. I'm a lawyer." Walsh dug a business card out of the inside pocket of his suit coat; approaching the boat, he offered it to Dean. Dean peered at the card, making out Walsh's name and, beneath it, the words *Attorney at Law*.

When it dawned on Walsh that Dean wasn't going to take the card, he shoved it back in the pocket. "I represent the grandmother of one of those kids you pulled out of the drink the other night—Agatha Pierce Campbell, of the Newport Campbells. She's known for her philanthropic—"

"Yeah, I've heard of her."

"Mrs. Campbell is extremely grateful to you for having saved her grandson's life. She's asked me to demonstrate that gratitude by giving you a million dollars, free and clear." Walsh held up the green envelope. "I've seen to all the legal hoo-ha and taken care of the taxes. All you have to do is sign a few papers, take the check, and you're a million dollars richer. Not bad in exchange for freezing your butt off in ice water for ten minutes, no?"

Ten minutes? It had taken days for the chill to leave Dean's bones.

He frowned at the green envelope. This couldn't be for real.

"Look." Walsh buttoned up his trench coat with red, quivering fingers. "Speaking of butts freezing off, I'm not exactly dressed for the weather here. Why don't you just do us both a favor and take the damn letter. Please."

After a moment's hesitation, Dean hopped down onto the dock, took the envelope from Walsh and ripped it open. Inside was the promised million-dollar cashier's check made out to him. "What's the catch?"

"No catch. Except—" Walsh retrieved some official-looking forms and a pen from his briefcase "—you've got to give me your John Hancock in about half a dozen places, and the money is yours. This is a gift, plain and simple. All you have to do is figure out how to spend it."

A million dollars; it wouldn't make him rich, not by today's standards, but it was a tidy little chunk of change. If there was any one thing about Dean's life that he would change if he could, it would be the on-going need to raise funds to keep the *Lorelei* afloat and put food in his belly. Summers weren't too bad; he generally had all the charter business he could handle. But this time of year was rough; every time the money started drying up, he had to bang out another magazine article on his battered old manual typewriter with the sticky *P*.

No, that was wrong. There was something else he would change if he could. Or rather, there was something he would have done differently six years ago, a mistake he would have avoided so that he wouldn't have to live forever with a memory that shamed him to his bones.

It wasn't just what he'd done that long-ago night that filled him with remorse; it was all the years since then. It was having to live with knowing what kind of a man he really was—the kind who could promise his best buddy, as he lay dying, that he'd look after his wife, and then...

Dean swore under his breath and dragged a hand through his hair, ignoring George Walsh as he thrust the pen and papers toward him.

And then there was that night, the night Dean wished to God had never happened, although from time to time he awoke sweating and trembling and breathing Laura's name after reliving it in his dreams.

There was that night, and then there were the six years since, six long years during which he'd tried to forget what he'd promised Will Sweeney after a truck bomb had demolished their barracks in Dhahran and carved a hole in Will's chest.

"I'll take care of her," he'd sworn—and meant it. After all, Laura had been his friend since their freshman year at Rutgers, just as Will had. Dean would make sure she was provided for, that she'd always have a roof over her head and enough money to get by, and that no harm would ever come to her. But Will had put his faith in the wrong man. He should have known Dean would just screw things up.

For six years Dean had left her on her own, neglecting his promise because he couldn't face her after that night. He'd told himself it was for her own good, but the bottom line was, if he hadn't messed up so bad, he might have had the guts to stick around and keep his promise to Will. He would have been able to look after her, not just hope she did okay on her own.

She *had* done okay, she and her daughter, according to that P.I. he'd hired a couple of years back to check up on her—but just barely. She supplemented her Social Security and military survivor benefits by painting seascapes, but the income from that kind of thing was modest and sporadic. Dean knew money was an ongoing struggle for her, but though he would have liked to help her out financially—in part, as recompense for how unconscionably he'd acted the last time he'd seen her—he'd never had the means.

Until now.

"Kettering, for crying out loud." Walsh grabbed Dean's free hand and shoved the pen and forms into it. "Just sign this crap and take the check, so I can go."

Dean inspected the check. "Can you endorse a cashier's check to a third party, like with a regular check?"

"Sure, I guess, but..." Walsh frowned in evident bewilderment. "You want to give it to someone else? The whole million?"

"Yeah, I don't want it."

Walsh blinked at him. "You don't want it."

Dean clicked the pen. "Turn around."

"What?"

"Around." He gestured in a circular motion with the pen.

Walsh pivoted slowly, his expression dubious. Dean stuck the green envelope and the check between his teeth, flattened the forms down on Walsh's back, signed them and handed them to the lawyer.

Walsh handed a couple back, saying, "These are for you," and stowed his copies in his briefcase with a sigh of relief. "Thank you, Mr. Kettering. It's been a pleasure—"

"Stay put." Slipping the forms in his pocket, Dean

laid the check facedown on Walsh's back, wrote "Pay to the order of Laura Sweeney" on the reverse side and signed it. "Here." He handed the lawyer the check.

"Uh..." He turned it over in his hand. "Why are you giving this to me?"

"So you can deliver it for me."

"*Whoa!*" Walsh wheeled around, but Dean grabbed him and faced him away again.

"Hold still," Dean ordered. "You'll need to know where she lives." Holding the green envelope against Walsh's back, he wrote Laura's name and address on it.

"Look, *pal*," Walsh said, "my job was to give *you* the check, and now I've done that, so—"

"I'm not asking you to hand-deliver it," Dean said. "You can send it by courier, mail it, whatever...."

"So can you."

"I'd rather it went out from your office." If Dean knew Laura, her first impulse would be to return the money, but she could only do that if she knew where he lived. Any guaranteed postal or courier service would display his return address right there on the outside of the package. He handed Walsh the envelope and pen.

"You know," Walsh said as he slid the check back into the envelope, "it's risky entrusting a cashier's check this size to a courier service. You really want to deliver something like this in person. She lives where?" He squinted at the address Dean had written on the envelope. "Seven Cliffside Drive, Port Livingston, New York?"

Dean nodded. "It's this little village on the north shore of Long Island." He'd always liked Port Liv, one of those quaint old waterfront communities with way too many antiques shops and tourist traps, but a pretty good marina. According to the P.I.'s report, Laura lived in what used to be her grandmother's summer place, an old stone cottage covered with ivy, where Dean and Will and Laura used to spend blissful long weekends away from the demands of college and, for Will and Dean, Air Force ROTC—Reserve Officers' Training Corps.

"Well, I'm not going all the way to Long Island," Walsh said. "But maybe you should."

"Not an option."

"You sure? 'Cause it's really not safe, sending a cashier's check by—"

"Real sure."

"Just so you understand I'm not liable if anything goes—"

"Understood."

Walsh shrugged. "Suit yourself. I'll overnight it today." Nodding toward the *Lorelei*, undraped and basking in the wintry sun, but still almost completely iced in, he said, "Is it true you live on that thing? Year-round?"

Dean nodded. "That's right. I spend my summers sailing and my winters here in this marina."

"Seriously? I mean, it must be cool in the summer, but I think I'd go squirrelly spending my winters all alone on that thing, surrounded by ice."

"You wouldn't do it in the first place if you weren't already completely toasted."

Walsh's shaggy eyebrows quirked. "What do you know. The Ancient Mariner has a sense of humor."

I did once, Dean thought, remembering how it was back in college, cracking jokes with Laura while Will laughed his ass off. Resolving to lighten up on Walsh now that he'd agreed to send the check to Laura, Dean forced a smile and said, "What's this 'ancient' stuff? Do I look that old to you?"

Walsh studied him for a long, solemn moment. "Your eyes do."

Dean's smile faded.

The lawyer squinted at the writing on the green envelope. "Laura Sweeney," he murmured. Extending the envelope toward Dean, he said quietly, "Are you sure you don't want to bring this to her yourself?"

"Yeah." Dean shoved his hands in the back pockets of his jeans. "I'm sure."

With a weighty sigh, Walsh shoved the envelope into his briefcase and zipped it up. "It's been real, Kettering," he said over his shoulder as he turned and trudged away.

Reaching into his back pocket, Dean pulled out his wallet and withdrew the time-weathered photograph he kept tucked in its own little slot. It was a wallet-size studio portrait of Laura and Will dressed for their wedding, Will smiling proudly in his dress blues, Laura more incandescent than ever in that simple white gown, her honeyed-silk hair crowned by a wreath of daisies. Will's mother had tried to talk her into rosebuds, or lilies, or orchids, protesting that daisies lacked a certain cool sophistication, to which

Laura had replied that *she* lacked a certain cool sophistication, and that daisies suited her just fine.

They had. She'd looked astonishing that day, pristine and bewitching, her eyes—those soulful amber eyes—alight with pleasure. Her joy had been almost painful to behold; never had Dean felt so acutely empty.

Dean slipped the photograph carefully back into its slot, closed the wallet and shoved it back in his pocket.

A million dollars. It wasn't enough, not by a long shot. But it would have to do.

"YOU LOSE YOUR WAY or something?"

The ruddy-cheeked young FedEx guy on Laura Sweeney's front stoop kept his polite smile in place, but cocked his head. "Ma'am?" he said, expelling a cloud of vapor that hovered in the frigid air.

"You need directions?" asked Laura, who had never until now seen a Federal Express truck pull up in the driveway of the remote stone cottage she had called home for the past five years. Glancing down at the oversize envelope in his hand, she said, "What address are you looking for?"

"This one, I think." The young man held up the envelope. "This is 7 Cliffside Drive, right?"

Laura frowned at her name and address typed into the "To" section of the waybill in the plastic pouch on the front of the envelope. Under "Sender's Name" it said George Walsh, Attorney at Law, and underneath that an address in Newport, Rhode Island.

"I think there must be some sort of mistake," Laura said.

"Are you Laura Sweeney?" he asked.

"Uh, yeah, but—"

"Then there's no mistake." He clicked a pen and handed it to her, along with a clipboard. "Just sign right here if you would." Sniffing the warm, sweet aroma wafting out of Laura's kitchen in the back of the house, he added, "Smells great in there."

"We're making oatmeal cookies. You want one?"

"Raisins?"

"Yeah."

"Nah."

"Ooh, FedEx!" Laura's best friend, Kay, came into the front hall from the kitchen, brandishing a spatula. With her great cloud of wiry, prematurely gray hair and her batik caftan, Kay looked like the Wicked Witch of Haight-Ashbury. "Who's it from?"

Laura shrugged as she signed her name. "Some lawyer in Rhode Island."

"Don't accept it!" Kay snatched the pen out of Laura's hand. "You're probably being sued."

The FedEx guy blinked at Kay and then at Laura.

"Kay, honestly." Laura gestured toward herself, clad today in her Suzy Homemaker uniform of baggy jeans and flowered apron. "Who'd want to sue *me?*"

"You never know," Kay said. "People sue over the craziest things nowadays. There are all kinds of nuts in the world."

"You should know." Laura grabbed the pen back and completed her signature, then accepted the envelope and closed the door on the swiftly departing FedEx guy. Turning the nine-by-twelve-inch cardboard envelope over in her hands, she said, "How does this thing open?"

"There's a little strip you pull," Kay said as the kitchen buzzer went off. "I'll do it." She handed Laura the spatula and plucked the envelope out of her hand. "You get that batch out of the oven. The last one almost burned."

In the homey little kitchen, with its herb-festooned rafters and gingham curtains, Laura found her daughter, Janey, crossing to the antiquated oven, her bulbous tyrannosaurus-head slippers bobbing beneath the hem of her adult-size apron. The apron, like her face and blond braids, was liberally dusted with flour.

"No, you don't," Laura scolded as Janey reached for the handle of the oven door. "You know you're not allowed to open that." She turned off the timer and grabbed two oven mitts.

"But I'm a big girl now. You *said*. I'm five."

"Barely." Janey's fifth birthday was New Year's Day. "You need a little more experience being five before I let you start reaching inside hot ovens. Now stand back while I get these cookies out."

"I don't get to do *anything*," Janey muttered, folding her arms and thrusting her lower jaw out to drive home the magnitude of her displeasure; if it weren't for the big-eyed dinosaurs on her feet, she might almost have pulled it off.

"You got to mix up the dough." The door of the fifty-year-old oven screaked as Laura pulled it open, releasing a whoosh of cinnamon-scented heat; the cookies looked perfect. "And you got to taste-test the first batch. I'll let you test this one, too, once they're cool enough to eat."

Kay, holding a letter and a green envelope, appeared in the kitchen doorway as Laura withdrew the sheet of fragrant cookies. "Laura, check this out! Some guy named Dean Kettering is giving you a mil—"

Laura dropped the pan with a harsh clang onto the slate floor. Some cookies slid off; most broke.

Janey gasped.

Laura stared at Kay for a long, incredulous moment. "Did you say Dean Kettering?"

"Uh...yeah."

Laura held out her hand. "Give that to..." With a little growl, she yanked off her oven mitts and tossed them at the big, scarred pine table that took up most of her homey little kitchen; they missed the table and landed on the floor. "Give that to me."

Kay handed over the letter and envelope with a wary expression, then retrieved the oven mitts and picked up the pan of cookies. "Janey, honey, why don't you gather up those broken cookies in that bowl so we can throw them outside for the birds?"

"Who's Dean Kettering?" asked Janey as she squatted down to collect the cookie bits, her trouble with *r*'s making his last name sound like "Kettle-wing."

Kay cast Laura a significant look as she set the cookie sheet on the stovetop, one eyebrow raised in a silent echo of Janey's question.

"He's..." *Oh, God.* Laura took a deep breath and made herself smile at her daughter. "He's an old friend of...your father's. And mine."

Janey's luminous blue eyes grew wide. Kay knew

why. The child, having been born long after the terrorist attack in February 1995 that killed Will Sweeney,
had rarely heard the phrase "your father." Laura, who
was fanatical about one thing in life—honesty—made
it a habit to avoid saying those words. To say them
now, in this particular situation, made her cringe inside.

"Laura, are you okay?" Kay, who never missed a
nuance, tucked a wayward strand of hair behind
Laura's ear, then wiped at her cheek, which she'd evidently smeared with flour.

"You okay, Mommy?" asked Janey as she set her
bowlful of cookie shards on the table. She looked as
concerned—and as eerily astute—as her "aunt" Kay.

"I'm fine," Laura mumbled as she read the one-
sentence letter from George Walsh, Esquire, inform-
ing her simply that Dean Kettering had instructed him
to forward the enclosed cashier's check for one million
dollars, endorsed to her. She studied the green envelope, a bittersweet ache squeezing her chest as she
read her name and address written in Dean's distinc-
tive, jagged scrawl.

The envelope had already been ripped open. She
reached inside and slid out a check—it was a cashier's
check made out to Dean Kettering, she saw—in the
amount of...

Holy moly, it really was a million dollars. Shoving
the envelope in the back pocket of her jeans and flip-
ping the check over, she found that Dean had, indeed,
endorsed it to her.

Kay let out a long, impressed whistle when she saw
the check. "Is it for real?"

"Looks that way."

"Who *is* this guy?"

"He's an old friend," Laura said woodenly.

"A fwend of my daddy's," Janey elaborated as she shuffled toward them.

"Must be a pretty rich fwend of your daddy's," Kay murmured, peering at the check with an incredulous expression.

"But he's not," Laura said. "Or he wasn't. Maybe he is now."

"Let me see!" Janey snatched the check out of Laura's hand and held it up to her face.

"When's the last time you saw this guy?" Kay asked.

"Almost six years ago," Laura answered. "April second, 1995. He came here to…" She darted a glance toward her daughter, who was mimicking Kay by examining the check with feigned fascination; or maybe she *was* fascinated. Janey found the damnedest things interesting. "He came to bring Will's things back to me—his belongings, our correspondence to each other…."

"Oh…oh, right," Kay said. Laura and Kay hadn't known each other when Will was killed. It was the following winter, shortly before Janey was born, that Kay had moved in next door and turned the old Sullivan place into the Blue Mist Bed and Breakfast.

Laura wrapped her arms around herself. "After Will died, I came here to be alone for a while and get my head together. Grandma was still alive, and this was her summer place, but the season hadn't started yet, so no one was around—no tourists, no family. I'd been here for a couple of months when Dean showed up one day, out of the blue. There was no phone service here then, so he couldn't call ahead."

"You knew him?"

Laura nodded. "We'd been friends in college. Good friends. He's was Will's roommate—his best buddy. The three of us were inseparable." A kaleidoscope of memories assailed her—she and Will and Dean playing touch football with some of the other ROTC guys and their girlfriends in the cold November mud...driving out here on weekends to sail the little cat Grandma Jane had given her, she and Dean showing a reluctant Will the ropes...trading jokes and mock insults with Dean over pitchers of beer while Will howled with laughter....

Then there were all the times she'd glance toward Dean, only to find him looking at her, his radiant eyes shadowed with something dark and unguarded, something they both felt but knew they must never acknowledge....

There was Dean's terrible remoteness the day she'd married Will and he'd served as best man, the way he wouldn't meet her eyes or speak to her...until the ceremony was over and he'd kissed her cheek, whispering, "I'm trying to be happy for you," the closest he'd ever come to saying it out loud....

And then there was the afternoon, not quite two years later, when Dean had shown up here in his sunglasses and his air force uniform, Will's personal effects in a cardboard box under his arm.

"And you haven't seen him since then?" Kay asked.

Laura looked away and shook her head.

"Why not? I mean, if you were such good fr—"

"Janey, give me that." Laura snatched the check out of her daughter's hand. "I can't keep this. I have to give it back."

"Well..." Kay contemplated the check with an ambivalent expression. "You might want to do some investigating. Sometimes you *should* look a gift horse in the mouth. Find out what this guy is up to. I mean, who'd give a million bucks out of the blue to someone they haven't seen in six years? What does he want for it? You might have to give it back, but if it turns out he's on the level—"

"No. I can't take it under any conditions. I couldn't live with myself. It just...it wouldn't be right."

"I don't know about *that*," Kay said. "I mean, I can't see where you'd be doing anything *wrong* by taking the money. It's just that you have no idea what this guy's agenda is. You don't want to get yourself obligated to some wacko from your past just 'cause he's decided to dump some bread on you. But if there really are no strings..."

"Forget it," Laura said resolutely.

"You're giving back the million dollars, Mommy?" Janey asked plaintively.

Laura groaned inwardly. "Yes, sweetie, I think so."

"But if you had a million dollars," Janey said, "you could buy Mr. Hale's boat, the one you showed me. You said if you could ever afford it, you'd buy it and then we could go sailing. You *said*."

"Sweetie..." Laura shook her head in exasperation. "You wouldn't understand it. It's a grown-up thing."

"I understand grown-up things," Kay said. "Try me."

"Kay, no. It's personal. Don't ask me to explain it."

"Look." Kay took the check out of Laura's hand. "You don't need to make this decision right now. Think about it. Call the guy up. Find out why he's—"

Laura grabbed the check back. "I don't need to think about it, and I have no intention of reestablishing contact with Dean Kettering. I don't want the money, and that's that."

Kay's all too perceptive gaze zeroed in on her. "Am I hearing this from the same woman who just yesterday was whining about how she was going to end up with carpal tunnel from clipping coupons? How long has it been since you've sold a painting, Laura? Weeks? Months?"

Laura rolled her eyes. "How long has it been since you've had a guest in your B and B? It's *March*, Kay. Both of us rely on seasonal income, and that's why we both store our nuts in the summer, like good little squirrels. Come Memorial Day, the tourists will flock back to Port Liv and you and I will be grousing about how we don't have enough time to spend all the money we're making."

"No, we'll be socking it away for the winter. Don't try and BS me, Laura. You've never been any good at it."

"What's BS?" Janey interjected.

Laura and Kay stared at the child. She looked back and forth between them, patiently waiting for an answer.

"It's short for bullshit," Laura told her.

Janey giggled and slapped her hand over her mouth, clearly astounded; Laura never swore in front of her. "Mommy said a bad word!"

Kay groaned. "Laura, you know, this unremitting honesty of yours gets to be a bit much sometimes. Do you always have to tell everybody the truth? Even a little kid?"

"I'm not little anymore!" Janey protested. "I'm five!"

"Yes." Squatting down, Laura wrapped her arms around Janey and squeezed her tight. "Especially if it's *my* kid. I love this little monkey too much to—" she winked at Janey "—BS her."

Janey shrieked with laughter. Pulling away from her mother, she ran into the living room, scratching under her arms and screeching like a chimp jazzed on double espressos. Laura heard her jumping around on their old, rump-sprung couch.

Kay adopted that smart-ass look that always made Laura want to slap her. "Do you love her enough to take the million dollars for her?"

Laura stood up with a little groan. "That's not fair, Kay. You don't know the whole story."

"Then tell me the whole story. Since when have I been a bad listener?"

Laura closed her eyes and rubbed her forehead with the hand holding the check. It smelled like money.

She could buy a dishwasher finally, and replace the roof so they'd be assured of getting through next winter without a major disaster. She could have a furnace put in so they didn't have to rely on that inadequate little woodstove. She could buy a new couch. Hell, with a million bucks, she could redecorate the whole place, get rid of Grandma's shabby old hand-me-downs....

Except she kind of liked all this ponderous old furniture. It was a comforting, ongoing reminder of her grandmother, who had brought her up since the age of two, when her parents had perished in a nine-car pileup during an ice storm. Grandma Jane had been her only family, her salvation, her entire world—a world Laura was loath to discard any part of, including Grandma's big, squishy chairs and lumpy behemoth of a couch. But maybe she could get them reupholstered so she could quit using bedsheets as slipcovers.

She could rid herself of that rust bucket she'd been driving around since college, and buy a real car.

She could fix the front porch, which was threatening to cave in if someone breathed on it hard.

She could start a college account for Janey.

And yes, she could buy that sleek little five-year-old Precision 18 that Raleigh Hale was asking $8,700 for. She could teach Janey to sail. Janey loved the water.

She could treat Janey—and herself—to some of life's luxuries for a change, not just scrape by with the necessities. And she could buy them both a little much-needed security in the bargain.

If she were willing, that was, to take Dean Kettering's million dollars. Why was he giving it to her? What, after all these years of no contact at all between them, was he trying to prove? He'd had six years to mull over what happened. Maybe he was finally feeling guilty.

That must be it. He was feeling guilty—about that night, or the intervening years of silence, or both. God knew where he'd gotten that money, but he intended to use it to ease his conscience.

If it had begun and ended there, Laura might have been tempted to take the money. Hell, she *was* tempted to take it, sorely tempted. But there were too many reasons to turn it down, not the least of which was that she had a conscience, too. How could she rationalize taking a million dollars from Dean Kettering after the secret she'd been keeping from him for six years?

Laura folded the check and slid it into her jeans pocket next to the envelope. Crossing the kitchen, she grabbed her parka off its hook by the back door. "Keep an eye on Janey for me, okay?"

"Going somewhere?"

"Just down to the beach for a walk." Laura zipped the parka up over her apron.

"In this weather?"

She kicked off her slippers and crouched down to work her ragwool-socked feet into her duck boots. "It's nice and sunny."

"But cold."

Laura glanced up as she hitched the laces of her right boot tight in their eyelets. "It's March, Kay. Can't hibernate inside forever just 'cause it's still a little nippy." She retrieved her knit hat out of her pocket and pulled it on. "I just...I...I need a little air. I just need to..." A frustrated sigh escaped her.

"Sure, kiddo. Take your time. Think this thing

through. Don't make any decisions you're going to regret later."

Regret, Laura mused as she opened the back door, was something she'd learned to live with a long time ago. Kay couldn't tell her anything about regret.

Her boots crunched on the snow-glazed lawn as she carefully made her way toward the wooden staircase that led to the boulder-studded beach. A frigid breeze gusted off the water, fluttering her jacket and cutting right through her jeans. She strolled back and forth in the damp sand at the edge of the water, dodging incoming waves as she thought about the check in her pocket and the reason she couldn't keep it.

Facing away from the water, she shielded her eyes against the dazzling morning sun and peered up at the fairy-tale two-story stone cottage overlooking the Sound, which six years ago had belonged to Grandma Jane, and in which Laura had taken refuge after that nightmarish week in early February 1995.

First had come the news about Will, leaving her reeling with grief. Sweet, kind, dependable Will Sweeney, with his copper-penny hair and hearty laugh...Will Sweeney, with whom she'd expected to make babies and to grow old, was gone in a roaring explosion halfway around the world.

He'd been in the service. Even though they hadn't been at war, she'd always known there were risks. Given her lifelong fear of flying, it had especially freaked her out that he'd chosen the air force; it wasn't terrorist truck bombs she'd fretted about, but the possibility that one of those fighter jets would crash, taking him with it. Will used to assure her it was safe, and she'd wanted to believe him, wanted to be as confident as he that it could never happen. Not to Will, who'd never let her down, never let anyone down, who'd always been there for everyone, solid and reliable.

Yet he was gone, just like that. She'd never see him again.

Then, the day after the memorial service, her just-begun pregnancy had ended in a miscarriage that may or may not have been brought on by the stress of Will's death. She'd told him she was expecting just days before, in a letter he'd never even had the chance to read. If he'd known, as he lay dying, that they were going to have a baby, would it have been any comfort to him?

First she'd lost Will. Then she'd lost the baby. Within the space of a week, everything important to Laura had been torn away from her. It hadn't taken her long to grow weary of the ceaseless condolences, the pitying looks—although only Grandma Jane had known about the miscarriage; no one else had even known she was pregnant. She'd needed sanctuary, and Grandma had, as always, come through, with the offer of her summer cottage, blessedly empty.

Laura had gratefully holed up here, where there was no phone, no television, not even any neighbors, the old Sullivan place—the only house visible from the cottage—having stood empty for two years. She'd occupied her days painting the violent splendor of Long Island Sound and her nights reading her way through Grandma's vast collection of tattered paperbacks.

As the weeks passed, her wounded soul had gradually begun to knit, a sense of grudging acceptance settling in to replace the trauma of losing Will and the baby. The joy of sketching and painting had sustained her, giving her something to focus on besides the pain, something to think about and plan and carry out.

Some days she'd even felt a fleeting sense of peace, an awareness that she was strong and whole and that she would survive this, she would move on and build a life for herself out of the ashes of this tragedy. She might even fall in love again someday, get married and grow large with some other man's child. Other women might crave dazzling careers and high-powered lives; Laura Sweeney's most heartfelt aspiration had always been to settle down and raise a family. It was her destiny, her fondest desire.

The quiet and solitude of Grandma's cottage had been just what she'd needed—yet, at the same time, she'd never felt more alone, more empty, more needful of human companionship. Lying in her lonely bed night after night, she had begun to feel as if it had been years since she'd been touched.

Laura didn't often think back to that time; she'd moved beyond the sorrow and saw no point in dwelling on it. Now, reliving those dreamlike weeks, she wondered whether it was the bitter wind or her memories making her eyes sting with tears.

The cottage and the stairway leading up to it wavered through a watery haze. At the top of the stairs, she saw the spectral form of a man, tall and severe in his blue air force uniform, his eyes concealed behind the blackest of sunglasses, a cardboard box tied with string tucked beneath his arm.

She blinked and the image was gone in a hot spill of tears. *He* was gone.

Dean Kettering. That's how she'd first seen him that April afternoon six years ago when he'd come to bring Will's things to her. She'd been about a hundred yards down the beach, sketching details of surf exploding against rocks for the monumental painting she'd embarked on. But as the golden afternoon light had begun to dim, she'd grown chilly in her jeans and sweatshirt, and had decided to pack it in. As she headed back to the stairs, juggling her toolbox full of drawing supplies, her easel and her big sketch pad, she'd looked up and seen him, just standing there on the top step, gazing down at her.

She wondered how long he'd been watching her....

2

"DEAN." Laura had heard the surprise in her voice. She hadn't seen Dean Kettering since he and Will had shipped out to Saudi Arabia in January. He'd been unable to come home for Will's memorial service.

He took off his sunglasses and slipped them into an inside pocket of his jacket, which was unbuttoned. The breeze flipped his tie over his shoulder, but he didn't seem to notice. His eyes, shadowed by the brim of his cap, were luminescent. Softly he said, "Hey, Lorelei."

Lorelei. It had been his pet name for her all through college. "She was a siren who haunted the Rhine," he'd told her, "trailing a golden comb through her hair while she sang a song of savage beauty, luring boats to destruction on the rocks and rapids." The joke, springing from Dean's well-known contempt for the institution of marriage, was that Laura had used her sirenlike charms to entice Will Sweeney into a life of domestic docility, a fate worse than that of the sailors and fishermen who'd fallen prey to the Lorelei of legend. It had been good-natured teasing, or so she'd always assumed. She'd never been entirely sure about anything when it came to Dean Kettering.

As Laura approached the staircase, Dean set his box on the ground and sprinted down to assist her, taking the easel and sketch pad from her and following her up the steps.

At the top, she glanced down at the box, a small corrugated carton wrapped in rough twine. "What's that?"

Dean bent to lift the box, tucking it under the same arm that held the easel and pad. "Some of Will's things. Letters and the like. I thought you'd want to have them."

She met his gaze for a moment, then looked away and nodded. "Did you just fly in?"

"Yeah, I'm on leave."

"Are you hungry? Can you stay for dinner, or do you have somewhere you have to be?"

"You mean, do I have an itinerary? Me?"

She forced a smile. "Yeah, look who I'm talking to." She turned and started walking toward the house. "I've got some beef stew in the slow cooker, if you want some."

His footsteps were close behind hers. "Laura."

She didn't slow her pace. "'Cause there's plenty. I make it in big batches and freeze it for—"

His hand closed over her arm, stilling her. He came around to face her. "I'm sorry. About Will."

She nodded, not meeting his eyes.

"I should have called you," he said. "I just didn't know what to say. And I'm no good at notes and all that."

She gazed past him at the turbulent Sound. "It's all right. I got sick of everybody's sympathy." It wasn't all right, of course, but calling or sending a note would have been the thoughtful thing, and Dean Kettering had never been too good at doing the thoughtful thing. In college, he'd found certain women—those who were drawn to his feral, somewhat dangerous brand of masculinity—to be easy conquests, but once he ran them to ground, he generally dropped them without a word. He never officially broke up with anyone, never offered explanations; he just never called back.

Dean stroked Laura's arm, a comforting caress. It was the first time anyone had touched her in so long. She closed her eyes to savor the warm friction of his hand through her worn sweatshirt.

It was strange to feel Dean touching her like this. Back in college, they never used to touch. They'd avoided even the most casual contact, as if to do otherwise might pop open a Pandora's box of sublimated longing best left under lock and key.

There'd always been that awareness thrumming between them, making everything quiver slightly just under the surface. Will had been oblivious to it, thank God; Dean had been his best friend since freshman orientation, Laura his steady girlfriend for even longer, since their sophomore year of high school.

She used to worry that Dean would break down and put the moves on her someday—given the way he'd used women and tossed them aside, she'd half expected it—but apparently his bond with Will had kept any such impulses at bay. That had been fortunate for any number of reasons, not the least of which was that Dean, with his aura of reckless self-sufficiency, had scared her just as much as he'd intrigued her.

They were complete opposites, she and Dean Kettering. Everything about him was foreign to her. He was a lone wolf—restless, predatory, impulsive and utterly autonomous. Laura, on the other hand, could not have been more of a communal being. She craved the warmth of other bodies around her, the security of the family bond—as did Will Sweeney, which was why it had felt so right, so comfortable, being with him.

But now Will was gone, and she was alone again—frighteningly alone.

"Laura?" Dean's knuckles grazed her cheek. "Are you okay?"

Laura opened her eyes to find his face close to hers, his eyes filled with concern. She nodded and backed away from his touch. "I'm fine. Just a little..." She shook her head. "It's a little disorienting, is all—turning around and finding you here."

"I would have called if you had a phone. You want me to split?"

"No."

"I mean, I know you came here to be alone. I've got a car. Maybe I should just—"

"No, Dean." She touched his arm, then quickly withdrew her hand. "I'm glad you're here. It's good to have some company for a change. Come on inside. Let's eat."

Dinner was a subdued affair, their conversation sporadic and awkward—a striking contrast to how it always used to be between them, the bantering and wisecracking that would leave Will choking with laughter. That was it, she decided; Will wasn't there to complete them. Without him to act as an audience for them—and a buffer for whatever it was that simmered so stubbornly between them—Laura and Dean didn't quite know how to be together.

After dinner, she washed the dishes while he dried them and put them away; he knew where everything went, having spent innumerable weekends here with Laura and Will during their college years. Without looking up from the sink, she asked, "Do you have a place to stay tonight?"

"No itinerary, remember?"

"'Cause you can stay here, of course. I can make up the bed in the spare room, if you can deal with that lumpy old mattress. I remember how you used to complain about it."

"That was before I discovered air force cots. I don't mind the mattress, but…it's probably best that I head out. I don't want to be any trouble."

"You're not any trouble," she said, still without looking up.

"Sure I am." His voice was low and had a strange, almost ominous edge to it.

She did look up then, to find him standing closer than she'd realized, regarding her gravely. Pulling the plug out of the sink, she wiped her hands on a dish towel and headed upstairs. "I'll make up the bed."

When she came back downstairs, Dean handed her the cardboard box and went out to fetch his duffel bag from the car. As he stepped onto the front porch, he pulled a pack of Marlboros from his pocket.

She took the box into the little solarium on the south side of the house, which she'd turned into a painting studio, and set it on her worktable among cans of brushes soaking in turpentine and half-squeezed tubes of oil paint. The sun had set, so she flipped the switch, igniting the full-spectrum strip lighting overhead. Grabbing a drafting knife, she severed the cord that bound the box, took a deep breath and opened it.

The top half of the box was filled with letters in envelopes, most addressed to Will in her handwriting. They'd all been opened and read with the exception of one, from her, postmarked February 3, 1995, still sealed. Obviously it had arrived after Will's death.

Something compelled her to pick up her drafting knife, slit open the envelope and unfold the letter, which she'd written in India ink on a sheet of drawing paper and embellished with a border of baby booties, rattles and other icons of infancy.

"Dear Will," she'd written, "Remember that night we decided to throw away my diaphragm? Talk about beginner's luck..."

She dropped the letter back in the open box and turned away from it, wrapping her arms around herself. So. He hadn't known.

Eager to shift her thoughts away from Will and the baby, Laura approached her half-finished, way-too-big painting of Long Island Sound, supported by two side-by-side easels, and examined it critically. Parts of the shoreline were still just loosely sketched, but she'd blocked in the stormy violet-gray of the sky and the bottle green of waves erupting on the beach.

She opened her sketch pad to the drawings she'd executed on the beach earlier, retrieved a piece of willow charcoal from her toolbox and started filling in some of the details of surf striking the jagged boulders at the water's edge. As usual when she became absorbed in drawing or painting, she lost track of everything else—until she sensed that she wasn't alone, and glanced over her shoulder to find Dean leaning against the door frame, a bottle of red wine in one hand, watching her. He'd changed out of his uniform, she saw, into faded jeans and a black wool sweater topped by a denim jacket.

He nodded toward the painting. "It's like a giant bruise."

"Uh…"

"The sky, I mean." He walked into the room, studying the painting with quiet intensity. "It looks wounded. The water—" his gaze lit on the tempestuous waves crashing on the beach— "just looks furious. Like it's wild with rage. This painting doesn't know whether it wants to scream or cry. Lots of passion there, Lorelei."

She dropped her charcoal into the toolbox. "It's just a seascape."

Will never used to comment on her paintings, except to say, "That one *rocks*," or "Another triumph, beautiful," which was fine; his praise was always sincere and enthusiastic, if a bit vague.

Dean looked at her. "You've painted seascapes before. They didn't look like this."

"Too melodramatic?"

"No, not at all. It's…" He shook his head as he took in the immense canvas. "It's beautiful. But scary. When I look at it, I feel like I'm looking inside your soul."

"That's scary?"

He contemplated the painting grimly. "Right now it is."

Laura pointed to the bottle of wine he held—a pinot noir of impressive vintage, its bottle furred with dust, its cork already removed. "Plundering my grandmother's wine rack?"

"Will she mind?"

Laura shook her head. "She hasn't even been here since she broke her hip two years ago. And she just kept the wine around for guests—never touched it herself."

"Thoughtful of a teetotaler to keep something around for her friends to drink."

"A teetotaler?" Laura chuckled. "You never saw her work her way through a pitcher of Beefeater martinis. She just didn't like wine."

Dean's laughter startled her. It was so unexpected, given their grief and their uneasiness with each other, and so refreshing. He looked suddenly younger, unencumbered, the carefree Dean Kettering of old.

"I thought we could maybe bring this down to the beach," he said, holding up the wine bottle, "and take a walk."

They used to take nighttime walks on the beach during their weekends here, she and Will and Dean; those walks were among her most pleasant memories of those years. After a moment's hesitation, Laura said, "Sure. Sounds great. Let me get my sweatshirt."

They strolled down the moonlit beach, passing the bottle back and forth as they made small talk, mostly about sailing—their great shared passion. It was what

Dean missed most, being in the air force, he told her— that freedom to get on a boat and just leave the world and all its responsibilities behind, to be one with the primal rhythms of the sea.

"There's something I've always wanted to ask you," Laura said as they headed toward an outcropping of boulders—a familiar landmark that used to serve as the turn-back point for their walks. She perched on a flat-topped rock that was about waist high and tilted the wine bottle to her mouth, feeling the velvety-soft pinot warm her from the inside as it went down. "What's a wild and crazy guy like you doing in the military? I mean, it's strange enough that you even went to college, but accepting that ROTC scholarship? You and ROTC...the pieces never really added up for me."

Leaning a hip against the rock Laura sat on, Dean withdrew his pack of cigarettes, shook one out and lit it with a match. In the old days, she would have needled him about smoking. But this wasn't the old days, and the thought of trading barbs with Dean Kettering here in the dark while they drank from the same bottle of wine felt, in a way, sacrilegious.

Dean's cigarette glowed orange as he drew on it, gazing out over the water. Laura listened to waves shatter softly, one after the other, on the rocky beach. The salty breeze off the water penetrated right through her sweatshirt now that she wasn't moving; she tugged the zipper up to her neck, but it didn't help much.

"Forget I asked," Laura said finally, handing the

bottle to Dean. "It's a personal question. It's none of my business."

"Friends are allowed to ask personal questions." Dean took a long swallow from the bottle. "I don't mind. I'm just not sure what to tell you. You're thinking I joined the air force in spite of being kind of a screwup."

"I didn't say—"

"When, really, that's pretty much *why* I joined up."

Laura wanted to argue with him, to deny that she'd intended any slur to his character, but her tongue was stilled by the revelation that he seemed to think so poorly of himself. He'd always come off as self-assured, cocky even. Laura had never thought to hear him describe himself as a "screwup."

"Did I ever tell you about my dad?" he asked, passing the bottle back to her.

"Only that he left when you were a kid."

"Yeah, I was eleven."

"That must have been rough, having him just walk out on you and your mom that way."

"I only wish he'd done it years earlier." He took another long drag on his cigarette, looking away from her. The tobacco smoke blended, not unpleasantly, with the briny sea air. They should make a men's cologne that smelled like that, Laura decided.

"Was it that bad?" she asked, bringing the bottle to her mouth.

He shrugged. "Mostly it was bad for my mom. He was a real bastard, always running around with other women. And he went through millions of dollars of her money."

Laura choked on the wine. "Millions?"

Dean's mouth thinned in a kind of grim smile. "Her side of the family is Southampton royalty."

"Why did she marry him?"

"She was pregnant with me."

"Ah." She tried to hand him back the bottle, but he waved it away and took another drag on his cigarette.

"Three guesses why he married her," Dean said. "And no, it wasn't because he was overcome with the urge to do the right thing. He'd already fathered two children out of wedlock that I know of, and there were more after he married my mom."

"Wouldn't have anything to do with those millions, would it?"

"Give the lady a prize. The old man had expensive tastes, and he needed a bankroll for them. While they were married, he bought two airplanes, three houses, at least a dozen Italian sports cars and pounds of diamond jewelry, none of which my mother ever saw. What he didn't spend, he pissed away at Monte Carlo and Vegas. When it was all gone, he split for Europe and married some baroness, leaving my mother destitute."

"What about her family? Didn't they help her out?"

"Just enough to get by. Her parents had disinherited her when she married my father, but they took pity on her and set us up in an apartment in Westhampton after the divorce. They never let her forget it was charity, though. And they never let *me* forget that I had that bastard's blood in my veins. All through my adolescence, every time I colored outside the lines, they were on my back, reminding me what a congenital SOB I was."

"Some grandparents."

"No, they were right. I mean, they were Nazis, but they weren't stupid. They had eyes and ears. I was always getting separated from the pack and acting out. Only time I was cool was when I was sailing. My friends used to let me take their boats out, and I got hooked on it pretty early. But on dry land, I was a trouble magnet. I got arrested once, as a juvenile—drunk and disorderly."

"Seriously? I never knew that."

"It was my only brush with the law, but I always hated toeing the line, always had an itch to go off and do my thing, regardless of how it affected anyone else."

"That doesn't mean you're just like your father."

"Doesn't it? Genetics isn't just some looney theory, Laura. It's real—it's bone deep. Underneath it all, I'm just like my old man—aimless, self-indulgent."

Laura drained the wine bottle and set it next to her on the rock. "I'm confused. What, exactly, do your supposed character defects have to do with your joining the air force?"

"You know." He inhaled the last of his cigarette, crushed it on the rock and slipped the butt into his front jeans pocket. "It's like when the delinquent son gets sent to military school in the hope that some structure and discipline will straighten him out. Only nobody sent me. I sent myself."

"You thought you needed straightening out?" Laura couldn't help but smile.

Gravely Dean said, "Don't you?"

No easy answer leaped to mind. Laura couldn't deny that Dean would be better off if he settled down some. His plan to inject a little military starch into his personality wasn't really a bad one; in fact, it appeared to be working, to some extent. "You survived ROTC," she said. "And you made it through two years in the air force without going AWOL. If you were a bad seed, it would appear you've been cured."

He shook his head. "It's a constant struggle to keep playing by the air force's rules. One of these days I'm afraid I'm going to deck a superior officer, or just walk off the base without looking back. I'm a court-martial waiting to happen."

She rested a hand on his arm. They'd never talked like this—seriously, about things that mattered. "You're a better person than you think, Dean."

A funny little glimmer lit his eyes. "Will used to say that."

She withdrew her hand and wrapped her arms around herself, feeling the biting breezes more than ever.

Dean swore softly under his breath. "Sorry."

"For what?" She hugged herself, shivering. "For mentioning Will? He meant a lot to both of us. Why shouldn't we talk about him?"

"Because you're still too raw."

"No, I'm not."

"That painting says you are."

"You read too much into things. I'm fine."

He stroked her face, his fingers hot and rough against her cheek. "You're shivering."

"I'm just cold." She slid off the rock and stood facing him. "Maybe we should go back."

Dean whipped off his denim jacket and draped it over her shoulders. It had absorbed his body heat and was imbued, just faintly, with a scent that made her think of warm skin and hot breath and the weight of another body against hers.

He chafed her arms with both hands, drew her close and rubbed her back through the jacket. Warmth seeped through her, quickening her heart, just a little, enough to make her slightly breathless.

Dean cradled her head against his shoulder, his woolen sweater scratchy-soft against her cheek, his chest rising and falling in rapid counterpoint to the steady cadence of the waves.

His hands stilled. He stopped rubbing her, just gathered her to him and held her.

She returned the embrace, her arms encircling him instinctively, needfully.

He threaded his fingers through her hair, nuzzled her with his jaw. She felt his breath against her temple and a soft hot tickle that could only be one thing—a kiss.

A chaste kiss. Friendly. Brotherly, even. Still...

A little unsteadily she said, "We should really go back, Dean. It's late, and..."

"And you're cold." He sighed. "Yeah, I know." His arms tightened around her momentarily, and then he released her and turned around. She grabbed the wine bottle.

They walked back to the house in silence.

LAURA LAY AWAKE until well after midnight, listening to Dean walking around on century-old floors, first in his room across the hall, then downstairs.

When she heard the back door open and close, she got up and parted the curtains over the rear window. By the light of the full moon, she saw Dean walking away from her across the backyard. At the dropoff to the beach, he paused. Presently a tiny orange dot materialized, and she knew he had lit a cigarette. He descended the stairs, and she lost sight of him.

It was close to one when she heard him reenter the house. His footsteps creaked through the kitchen and up the stairs to his room. Sounds traveled in this old house at night. Lying motionless, she heard the soft scrape of a drawer opening, the grind of rusty hinges on the door of the closet in his room, a clatter of coat hangers.

His footsteps paused in the hallway outside her room, and then she heard them groaning down the old stairs. She shoved the quilt down and got out of bed, threw her robe over her flannel nightgown and opened her bedroom door.

Dean, halfway down the stairs, turned to look at her, his eyes scaldingly blue in the semidarkness, the only light being what came from his room. He had on his denim jacket and jeans. In one hand he held his duffel bag; in the other, his uniform on a hanger, thrown over a shoulder.

Even in the near darkness, she could see the remorse in his eyes, along with a hint of that remoteness she'd come to know—and hate—so well over the years.

Steadying herself with a hand on the doorknob, she said, "You weren't going to say goodbye?"

He looked away, then met her eyes again. "I didn't want to wake you."

"And of course, you don't believe in notes, so I would have just awakened in the morning and found you gone."

His jaw clenched. "Laura..."

"You say you want to change, you want to straighten out, and then you up and bolt in the middle of the night with no—"

"I can't stay here, Laura."

"Why?"

His eyes closed briefly. When they opened, they held a look of grim resolve that made her shiver.

He stalked up the stairs two at a time, his gaze locked on her.

She backed up into her room until she felt the foot of her bed against her legs.

He dropped his duffel and uniform on the landing, crossed to her in three long strides, wrapped his hands around her head and kissed her.

On the mouth this time, and hard. Too hard. It hurt. It shocked her, made her heart hammer wildly, every nerve in her body tighten with alarm...

And need.

She clutched at his jacket, not knowing whether to push him away or pull him close, horrified, thrilled, overwhelmed.

His hands gripped her skull like a vise as his mouth plundered hers, took it savagely, hungrily.

He released her and backed away, his chest pumping, his eyes mirroring the fierce panic rioting through her.

"Okay?" he rasped. "Now do you see why I have to go?"

"No, Dean," she found herself saying as he wheeled around and walked away. "You don't."

She thought he hadn't heard her, half hoped he hadn't heard her. But in the doorway he stilled, his hands fisted at his sides, and she knew he had.

A weighty moment passed, Laura knowing she should take it back, but too desperate, too filled with need, to say anything.

Dean turned and came to her.

3

"WORKING GIRL, Sabrina or *Six Days Seven Nights?"* Kay tossed the three videocassettes on the sofa next to Laura—the quaint burgundy velvet sofa in the front parlor of the big old gingerbread Victorian that served as Kay's home and livelihood. The Blue Mist Bed and Breakfast, which provided the only accommodations in Port Liv aside from a fairly cheesy motel on the edge of town, was always filled to capacity in the summer. During the winter, on the other hand, it was generally, as now, devoid of guests.

Every Thursday night from November through May was Chick Flick Night at the Blue Mist. At nine o'clock, Laura would tuck Janey into the high, canopied feather bed in the Rose Room—Janey's favorite among the B and B's five guest rooms—and then she and Kay would make up a bowl of popcorn, uncork a bottle of wine and select a film from the prodigious collection of videotapes Kay kept on hand for guests. Laura used to wake Janey up and bring her home afterward, but that had proved troublesome and ultimately pointless. Now she just spent the night and had breakfast with her aunt Kay in the morning, after which Laura came to collect her for preschool, which she attended on Mondays, Wednesdays and Fridays.

"Laura?" Kay prompted. "You were the one who asked for Harrison Ford tonight, so what'll it be?"

"How do I send something by Federal Express?"

"Either that's a complete non sequitur or Harrison Ford made some romantic comedy about a FedEx guy that I never heard of."

"Complete non sequitur. Tomorrow I'm going to return that million dollar check to the lawyer who sent it to—"

"No, no, no, no, no!" Kay shoved the cassettes aside and sat next to Laura on the sofa.

"Yes, yes, yes, yes, yes." Leaning forward, Laura grabbed the bottle of merlot off the coffee table and refilled her glass. "It's the only right thing to do." And the only smart thing to do.

"Look. Laura..." Kay squeezed her friend's hand. "I know you've got mysterious issues where this guy is concerned, and I know you think it's wrong for some reason to take this money. But it only just arrived this morning. You haven't really had time to think about it—"

"Yes, I have." Laura gulped down some wine.

"Or to digest what it would mean for Janey."

"Bringing Janey into it is a cheap shot, Kay. And not as clever a strategy as you might think. I'm returning the check."

"Why so hasty? Don't you want to talk to this Dean Kettering and find out why he sent it? I mean, if he doesn't expect anything in return, and it's just money out of the clear blue—"

"I couldn't talk to Dean even if I wanted to. I haven't got the slightest idea where he lives."

Kay shrugged. "Newport, Rhode Island, most likely. He used a Newport lawyer to send the money to you."

"Newport, Rhode Island—well, that narrows it down."

"You could call that lawyer on Monday and try to sweet-talk him into giving you the guy's address."

"Which he wouldn't do, especially if Dean is a client of his, but it's all academic, because first thing tomorrow morning I'm going to send that check right back to—"

"Look, Laura, I can get on my computer and find this Dean Kettering right now in about five minutes if you want."

"I don't want."

"Aren't you just the tiniest bit curious as to his whereabouts? I mean, he knows where *you* live."

"Yeah, well, he knows all about this house. He used to come here with Will and me all the time while we were in college, back when it was still Grandma Jane's summer place."

"Yeah, but how does he know it's your permanent home now? Apparently *he's* done some snooping. Now it's your turn." Standing up, Kay crossed the room and took a seat at the massive old oak desk that housed her computer, printer and fax machine. She pressed a button on the monitor and the screen crackled on; she hit a few keys and the computer produced a series of beeps and hisses that meant it was going online.

It was one of Laura's more shameful secrets that she did not so much as know how to turn a computer on, much less tap into or negotiate that enigmatic entity known as the Internet. Whenever she watched Kay do it, she was consumed by awe and bewilderment. Kay's fingers fluttered over the keys and whole worlds of information flickered past. She received and sent e-mail. She talked to people in chat rooms. She had even created, all by herself, a Web site for her bed and breakfast!

"Okay, this is a search engine for finding people," Kay said as keys rattled beneath her fingertips. "There are a couple of ways to locate them. Let's start by look-ing for his phone number." She punched a key and waited, then shook her head. "It's drawing a blank. Probably he's unlisted."

"Or maybe he doesn't have a phone." Laura found herself rising off the couch and wandering over to Kay's corner, grudgingly intrigued.

"Everyone has a phone."

"Dean Kettering's not 'everyone.' He's…" Laura took a pensive sip of wine.

"He's what?" Kay asked, amusement in her eyes.

Laura dragged another chair over to the desk and sat down. "No phone number. So, now what do you look for?"

Kay turned and grinned at her. "Ah, so you *are* cu-rious."

"Maybe—but wanting to know what became of him doesn't mean I intend to get in touch with him."

"Yeah, yeah, yeah. What I'm looking for now is an e-mail address." Kay entered some more keystrokes, but came up empty again. "Hmph. Maybe he's as computer-phobic as you are."

"I'm not phobic, just ignorant. There's a difference."

After trying three more people-search engines with no success, Kay pulled up a Web page with a banner that read Folkfinder. "Let's try this one. It's a last resort, because they charge a fee, but if he's got a street address within the United States, I guarantee you they'll come up with it."

"How much of a fee?" Laura asked fretfully.

"My treat." Kay entered Dean's name and probable state of residence. The machine mulled it over for about ten seconds, only to announce *No Results Found*.

Kay shook her head. "He's got to have a street address. Doesn't he?"

"Maybe he doesn't live in the U.S.," Laura offered.

"Then why did he use a lawyer from Newport? Does he come from there?"

"No," Laura said. "He grew up on Long Island— out in the Hamptons."

"The *Hamptons*." Kay's eyebrows shot up. "No wonder he can afford to throw million-dollar checks around."

"No, it wasn't like that. More of a riches to rags kind of scene. Dean's father blew all the money and then split when Dean was just a kid. He never would have been able to afford college if it weren't for his ROTC scholarship and this part-time job he had doing home repairs for a local contractor. Only reason he was able to learn how to sail was because friends took him out on their boats."

"He sails?"

"Oh, yeah, he's totally into it. Or was."

"That's something you two have in common, then," Kay observed, "that sailing bug."

"The only thing." What was it he'd said about genetics? *Underneath it all, I'm just like my old man—aimless, self-indulgent.*

Laura pictured Janey, fast asleep upstairs, her cheeks the color of the cabbage roses on the down comforter tucked around her, and felt a surge of maternal protectiveness that went bone deep. She was all Janey had. Sometimes the magnitude of that responsibility daunted her, and occasionally she wondered if Janey didn't suffer from not having a father around to provide a stabilizing male influence. Then she would remind herself that not all fathers fostered equilibrium in their children's lives. Some, like Dean's father—and Dean himself—were forces of turmoil in the lives of those who cared for them, especially when the time came for their big disappearing act.

There were, Laura reflected, some very compelling reasons she couldn't accept that million dollars.

"What do you think?" Kay pointed to the screen, where she'd pulled up a Web site called Newport Sailing Tours And Corporate Charters. Links for about a dozen charter outfits were listed on the site. "If he likes to sail, he might be running charters."

"Not impossible," Laura said, but as Kay methodically clicked on each link, scanning the pages for Dean's name—a long and laborious process—it became increasingly clear that this was just another dead end.

Kay sat back and flexed her fingers. "He's a hard man to track down, your Dean Kettering."

"This is a waste of time," Laura said. "Let's watch a movie. How about *Working Girl?* I could use a good Cinderella story." Ah, the fortifying power of fantasy.

"You kidding?" Sitting forward, Kay rubbed her hands together and attacked the keyboard again. "I'm just getting warmed up."

"Kay..." Laura groaned.

"This is the *Internet,* for crying out loud," Kay said as she typed. "There's not a human being alive who hasn't left his footprint *somewhere* on the Net. I *am* going to find him."

"Kay, you're really a pain in the butt when you get a fire in your belly—you know that, don't you?"

"Okay, what I'm going to do is just surf through Newport and see what materializes." Kay pulled up one site after another—Newport International Boat Show, Newport Real Estate, Newport County Chamber Of Commerce, Historic Mansions Of Newport... There were Web sites for lighthouses, marinas, vineyards, sailing schools, music festivals, and a ton of B and B sites, all of which Kay had to glance at, "just to see what the competition is doing."

Dean Kettering's footprint was nowhere to be seen.

Laura drained her wineglass. "I *have* mentioned that this is a total waste of time, haven't I?"

"Okay, it says here that Newport has, like, one newspaper, and it's a weekly. Let's check it out." Kay scrolled down the home page for *Newport This Week.* "Forget it. Can't do a search, and I'm not gonna read every article in the archives looking for 'Dean Kettering.' Lemme back out of here and try something else."

"Have I mentioned that this is way boring, too?"

With a weary sigh, Laura got up, went over to the coffee table and refilled her glass from the bottle there. "I'm gonna go into your kitchen and make some popcorn, and then I'm gonna boot up *Working Girl* and watch it all by my lonesome."

"Uh...Laura?"

"You can join me or you can just play computer geek all night. It's your—"

"Laura, you might want to come look at this." Kay aimed a self-satisfied smile over her shoulder.

Laura regarded her in silence for a moment, then returned to her seat in front of the computer.

"This is the Web site for the *Providence Journal*," Kay explained. "It looks to be the major daily in Rhode Island, and they let you do word searches of their local articles, only the past couple of days' worth, but—" she gestured toward the screen "—as you can see, we struck pay dirt. This appeared in the edition that hit the stands the day before yesterday—March 19."

A message on the screen read: *1 stories containing Dean Kettering.* That was followed by the headline of the article Kay had found, underlined to show that it was a hyperlink to the article itself: Portsmouth's Publicity-Shy Hero. There was a subheading beneath that: *Air Force vet pulls two Newport boys from icy water.*

"This is why I couldn't find him by surfing the Newport links," Kay said as she clicked on the link for the article. "He doesn't live in Newport—he lives in Portsmouth." Frowning, she added, "Only I thought Portsmouth was in New Hampshire."

"There's a Portsmouth in Rhode Island, too, small but with a bunch of marinas," Laura said, her gaze riveted on the screen as the text of the article appeared, along with a picture that materialized all too slowly, from top to bottom.

As the picture came into focus—a photograph of someone turning away from the camera with a hand held up—Laura at first thought it was a woman, because of the long, breeze-riffled hair. Then she noticed the width of the shoulders, the masculine way he held himself, and realized it was a man...but it couldn't be Dean.

"Is that him?" Kay asked.

"No." Laura sat forward to squint at the image as it coalesced, her gaze on the man's face—what little of it she could see through the unruly strands of dark hair blowing across it. It was a face both virile and aristocratic, with sharply hewn, almost too handsome features—a high-bridged nose, sculpted cheekbones, neon eyes—saved from cover-model perfection by that who-gives-a-damn hair and a remoteness in his gaze that said this was a man who'd been places and done things. "Oh, my God." Laura's heart jerked in her chest. "Yes. That's him."

"Yeah?" Kay whistled softly. "Kind of hunky...if you're into brooding, bad-boy derelict types, but they've never been my cup of tea."

"Mine, neither," Laura said a bit too quickly.

Kay glanced at her, a smile flirting with the corners of her mouth. Scrolling down the page, she said, "So, uh, this Dean Kettering was an old college pal of yours, huh?"

"Of mine and Will's."

"Uh-huh." Kay returned her attention to the screen,

where a second picture had appeared below the first—Dean's official air force portrait, complete with military razor cut and beribboned uniform. "Whoa, is that the same guy?"

"That's how he looked when I knew him," Laura offered. "I never imagined him with long hair."

"Are you checking this out?" Kay asked, pointing to the text of the article. "He saved two kids from drowning on the seventeenth." She read aloud from the article as Laura read along:

"It was four years ago that 29-year-old Portsmouth resident Dean Kettering received his honorable discharge from the United States Air Force, in which he served as first lieutenant, but it was Saturday night that he truly earned his hero's stripes. Two Newport youths, 15-year-old Evan Ashford and 16-year-old Brent Campbell, after leaving a Saint Patrick's Day celebration at a friend's home in Portsmouth at approximately 1:00 a.m., found themselves at Howell's Marina. On impulse, they untied a canoe belonging to the marina and paddled it into the Sakonnet River, where it capsized, plunging them both into the bitterly cold water. The boys, being inexperienced swimmers and intoxicated at the time, would likely have drowned had their screams not awakened Dean Kettering, one of Howell Marina's handful of winter 'live-aboards,' who was asleep on his sailboat when the mishap occurred. Mr. Kettering jumped into the river and swam in the dark through chunks of ice to the two boys, hauling them both to safety."

"Wow," Laura murmured.

"Okay, time out," Kay said. "Are they saying this guy lives on his sailboat? Year-round? In the winter in New England?"

"Evidently." Laura swiftly scanned the rest of the article. "Yeah, read farther down. It says he runs day charters in the summer and writes freelance articles for travel and sailing magazines in the winter."

"What kind of a lunatic spends the entire winter all alone on a sailboat surrounded by ice?"

Laura just sighed. No one had ever accused Dean Kettering of being conventional. Or sensible.

"So..." Sitting back, Kay lifted Laura's wineglass out of her hand and took a sip. "Where do you suppose the money came from?"

"Huh?"

"The million dollars he gave you." Peering at Dean's disreputable-looking "after" picture, Kay said, "Could it be ill-gotten gains? You think maybe he uses that boat of his to run drugs—something like that?"

Laura grabbed her wineglass back with a scornful roll of the eyes. "Dean Kettering is the last person in the world I would suspect of doing something like that."

"I dunno," Kay said, studying the picture. "He looks like a real wild card, if you ask me."

"Yeah, well, he is, to a point—or was. Back at Rutgers, Dean was...Will used to call him 'untamable.' For an ROTC guy, he was a real maverick, always raising some kind of hell with his superiors, then tearing around on his bike in the middle of the night—this awesome old 1973 Harley-Davidson Sportster. Once, when we were spending the weekend here, Will and I went looking for him in the morning and found him sleeping on the beach. He used to go off on his own a lot—disappear without a word and come back days later. When we asked where he'd been, he'd just shrug and change the subject."

"Off tom-catting in the middle of the night?"

"Maybe so, but no one girl could ever get a leash on him."

"So he had trouble walking the straight and narrow." Kay grabbed the wineglass back. "If you're trying to convince me he's incapable of running drugs for a living, you're going to have to do better than this."

"The thing you've got to understand about Dean is, underneath it all, he was pretty much a straight arrow when it came to the letter of the law. He never so much as took a hit on a joint the whole time he was in college. He's the last person I would expect to get rich from crime. Plus, if he were rich, I hardly think he'd be living on his sailboat—not year-round. It's got to be a brutal life in a lot of ways."

"Okay, you've sold me. He's not a drug dealer. He's an okay guy deep down inside, even if he does march to a different drummer." Pointing to the article on the screen, Kay said, "Hell, he's a hero. So why won't you take the money?"

"Can't we just say I have my reasons and leave it at that?"

"For the record, I hereby refuse to tell you how to send something by Federal Express."

"That's all right." Laura reappropriated her wineglass and took a slow sip as she studied Dean's picture—the new picture, with the long hair and the haunted eyes. "I'm not going to be sending the check to that lawyer."

"*Yes!*" Kay shot a fist.

"I'm going to bring it back to Dean myself. Tomorrow I'm going to drive up to Rhode Island and—"

"Nooo," Kay moaned, literally tearing at her steel-wool hair.

"'Fraid so. Listen, would you look after Janey while I'm gone? Tomorrow's Friday, so if you wouldn't mind driving her to preschool..."

"Laura..."

"I'll have to rent a car—my transmission is shot. And I guess I'll have to stay in a motel tomorrow night, so don't expect me back till Saturday afternoon." This little jaunt was going to set her back at least $150, Laura realized with dismay.

"You're crazy if you think I'm actually going to assist you in this insanity. Unless..." A devilish spark lit Kay's eyes. "One has to wonder about this sudden decision of yours to bring the check back personally instead of just returning it to that lawyer."

"Wonder all you want," Laura retorted, trying not to stare at Dean's image on the screen. "Do you have a map of New England? I don't think I do, and I've got to plan my route."

"A *map?* How utterly antediluvian, my dear. That's what trip planning software is for." Kay logged off and popped a disk into the CD-ROM drive. "So, you never answered me. How come you're bringing the check back to him yourself?"

Laura shrugged with forced nonchalance. "Maybe it's just the least he deserves after going to the trouble of sending it to me."

"Common courtesy, huh?" Kay asked with a skeptical smile.

"Something like that."

After a thoughtful moment, Kay reached for Laura's hand. "You can tell me, you know. Whatever it is, whatever this is really all about..."

"I know that, Kay. Just..." Laura squeezed her friend's hand and released it. "Not now. Not yet."

Kay nodded and punched a few keys; a map and some colorful text unfolded on the screen, accompanied by a tinny flourish of trumpets.

"Kay," Laura, said, "I really appreciate your helping me this way, even though you don't think I should be giving the money back."

"Don't be so quick to thank me," Kay said as she typed. "Seeing the way you react to him, I'm half convinced he's going to talk you into keeping the money."

"Impossible."

"Is it? Once you're face-to-face with him, after all these years...anything could happen." Kay cast Laura a shrewd little smile. "Anything at all."

4

LAURA STOPPED in her tracks on the snow-dusted pier when she saw him. He was standing on the deck of his sailboat, backlit by the rosy flush of a setting sun as he broke up ice off the port side with a boat hook.

An old salt who was a dead ringer for Popeye had pointed out the boat when she'd arrived at the marina after a brutal all-day drive from Long Island to Portsmouth, Rhode Island.

"Dean Kettering's moored down that away," Popeye had informed her, gesturing with his pipe toward the far end of the pier. "A fine wooden sloop he's got. Thirty-six feet. Calls her the *Lorelei*."

The *Lorelei?* It didn't mean anything, Laura told herself as she walked slowly down the pier, reading the names on the hulls of the iced-in boats. Dean had always been into the old legends. It wouldn't do to start reading meanings into things like that. She had a reason for being here, and when she'd done what she had to do, she'd turn around and go home.

And never seek him out again.

There it was. The *Lorelei*.

And then she saw him, hacking away at the ice with fierce determination. Unkempt hair fell around his face as he thrust the boat hook, wielding it like a weapon. In lieu of a jacket, Dean wore a big, blue woolen sweater with a ragged scarf wrapped around his neck.

She stared at him, her breath coming in icy gusts of vapor. Her ears burned from the cold; she pulled her hood up, wishing she'd brought a hat.

It *was* him. She recognized the squarded-off breadth of his shoulders, the length of his arms and legs, the controlled, strangely savage grace of his movements.

Laura jammed her hands—trembling despite her gloves—into the pockets of her parka. The check in its green envelope crackled in the righthand pocket.

This was a mistake. She should have couriered the check back to that lawyer. She shouldn't have come here.

Why had she?

Dean turned and looked at her, his eyes like blue fire in the ruddy dusk, the boat hook held poised like a spear. Unshaved, his hair lashing his face, he looked like a barbarian warrior poised for the kill.

Her heart thumped painfully in her chest.

Turn. Go.

He peered at her through his wind-whipped hair, his customary remoteness turned hard and impenetrable, his jaw set. She knew he couldn't see her face well enough to recognize her.

She withdrew a hand from her pocket and lowered her hood.

Several seconds passed. He reached up to rake the hair off his face. Softly, incredulously, he said, "Laura?"

She swallowed, nodded.

Dean lowered the boat hook slowly, his gaze never

leaving hers, his forbidding expression easing into one of dumbfounded recognition. He looked her up and down, taking in her utilitarian parka, jeans and duck boots.

His mouth softened. In a voice so low she could barely hear him, he said, "Hey, Lorelei."

A smile tugged at her lips, but she looked away before it could get the better of her. *Do what you've come to do and go.*

Pulling her righthand glove off, she burrowed into her pocket and produced the green envelope. "I came to give this back."

It wasn't until his eyes grew opaque again, and the line of his mouth severe, that she fully registered the pleasure that had buoyed his expression, if only momentarily.

He regarded her in that dark, intense way he had for a moment that stretched six years into the past.

She approached the boat, holding the envelope in her outstretched hand, now quivering noticeably. "Please take it."

Dean glanced at the envelope, set the boat hook aside and walked over to her. At the edge of the deck, he reached toward her. She thought he was going to take the envelope, but instead he closed his hand—clad in gray woolen gloves with the fingers cut off—firmly around her wrist. "Come down below."

"No." She tried to pull away from him, but he held tight. His sweater was faintly redolent of kerosene, its sleeves pushed up to reveal brown forearms roped with taut muscle. "Just take the check, Dean, please, and let me go."

"You're shivering," he said, rubbing her inner wrist with the pad of his thumb, coarse as sandpaper. "Come down below. I've got a pot of coffee on."

"Dean, please." She tried to twist out of his grip, but he was far too strong for that. "Just take the check and—"

"First the coffee." Seizing her other hand, he urged her toward him until she had no choice but to step off the dock and onto the boat. "Then we'll talk about the check."

Dean guided her with a hand on her back down the companionway and into his galley, where a battered old percolator bubbled away on the stovetop, infusing the small space with the heartening aroma of freshly brewed coffee. He peeled off his gloves and shoved them in the back pocket of his jeans, then pulled his blue sweater off over his head, revealing a threadbare gray sweatshirt underneath.

"You don't need that jacket down here," he said, holding a hand out.

Laura took her time removing her other glove and tucking them both away in a pocket of her parka, along with the check. "I'll keep it on. I'm not staying that long."

"Come on, it's eighty degrees in here." Dean took hold of the pull tab of her parka's zipper, causing her to flinch slightly, and drew it down. Meeting her gaze as he opened the heavy jacket and slid it off her shoulders, he said, "If you think you need armor to protect yourself from me, you're wrong."

Because he wouldn't try anything, or because there

was no protection from him? She let him take the parka and toss it aside, along with his sweater.

"It's just that I hadn't counted on this turning into a *visit*," she said as he retrieved two unmatched mugs and filled them with coffee.

She blinked at the cup he handed her, a thick, over-size mug with a hairline crack meandering through a picture of a Yankee whaler under full sail. Below it, in a quaint old typeface, was the legend World's Greatest Dad.

"It was cheap," he said in response to her non-plussed expression. "And I liked the boat."

Laura wrapped both hands around the mug to let its welcome heat seep through her palms and up her arms. "I just didn't intend this, you know? I mean, I only came here to give you back your check, not..." She shook her head in frustration at trying to explain herself. What was she doing here? This was a monu-mental mistake. She ought to have her head exam-ined.

"One and a half sugars and lots of milk, right?" He plunked a box of sugar, a quart of milk and a spoon on the counter and leaned a hip against it to watch her.

Laura sighed and occupied herself with stirring milk and sugar into her cup while she tried to ignore Dean's closeness, the brush of his arm against hers as he lifted his cup of scalding black coffee to his mouth, contemplating her as he took a sip. His head nearly touched the galley's low ceiling. It was too small for him in here, and way too small for both of them.

"Want to sit down?" Dean asked. "Or would that

be too much like a visit?" Not waiting for an answer, he turned and ducked through a doorway.

After a moment, Laura followed him, finding herself in a small cabin, homey and deliciously toasty. The pleasant tang of wood smoke scented the air, underscored subtly by hints of tobacco and kerosene. Looking around, she saw a fireplace mounted into the bulkhead at one end and a portable kerosene heater at the other.

"All the comforts of home." Dean pushed an old typewriter, a half-crushed pack of Marlboros and a scrawled-on legal pad to one end of a little table and set his coffee cup down. Reaching into a box beneath the fireplace, he grabbed a few short lengths of wood that looked as if they'd been salvaged off an old boat, and fed them into the flames. "Even if it is pretty much an ongoing battle to keep warm."

"I can relate," Laura said, looking around for a place to sit. The cabin's two upholstered benches were almost completely hidden beneath piles of books and papers. "I fantasize about having a furnace."

"You're still making do with that old woodstove?"

"That's right."

He shook his head. "It's a lot of work, keeping a whole house warm with that thing."

"I don't mind tending the stove. It's chopping up wood all winter that gets to me. My hands are so callused you wouldn't think they could still get blistered, but they do. I just had a cord delivered, and I can barely stand to look at it." She frowned as she took a sip of her coffee. "I was wondering—how did you know I was still living in Grandma Jane's cottage? A lot of years have passed since we last saw each other. I might have been living in Alaska, for all you knew."

The wood in the fireplace hissed and popped as Dean rearranged it with a poker. "Didn't you once tell me she'd left you that house in her will?"

"I couldn't have. I didn't even know about it till after she died, which was the summer after...I lost Will."

"How did she die?"

"A heart attack, and you're changing the subject."

"Bad habit of mine."

"No, it's not. Not that you don't have your share of bad habits..."

He smiled grimly. "The understatement of the millennium."

"But that's not one of them."

"A new addition to my repertoire of character defects. Don't let it be said that Dean Kettering doesn't know how to grow and change."

Laura rolled her eyes.

Dean turned to face her as he dusted off his hands. "Must have been hard on you, losing your grandmother, especially so soon after Will."

And the baby—the first baby—but the only person who'd known about her miscarriage was Grandma Jane.

"I coped," Laura said.

"You're good at that," Dean said. "You're very strong. I've always admired that about you—your capacity to tolerate whatever you had to tolerate, and not let it get to you."

Wanting to redirect the conversation, Laura looked

around and said, "Yeah, well, I'm not sure I could tolerate living the way you do—spending all winter in such a small space. Don't you get claustrophobic?"

"Nah. This is my cave. I hibernate in here all winter and make up for lost time when spring comes."

"You run charters, right?"

"Yeah, once I get back from Bermuda."

"Bermuda!"

"I sail there at the end of May for a couple of weeks of scuba diving, just to get the winter kinks out."

"Do you take on a crew?"

"God, no. Just me. Then I head back here and do the day charter thing for the rest of the summer."

"You never get lonely?"

"I'm no pack animal, Laura. You know that."

All too well.

"What about you?" he asked. "Do *you* get lonely?"

It seemed suddenly very still and close in the little cabin. "No—not really."

"Is there some guy in the picture?"

She shook her head. "I'm pretty much a homebody. But that doesn't mean I'm lonely. My best friend lives next door, and I see a lot of her. She used to be a psychologist, but then she decided she didn't believe in psychology anymore, so she decided to open up a bed and breakfast. Remember the old Sullivan place?"

"That big old Victorian monster?"

"Yeah, Kay bought it and turned it into a B and B called the Blue Mist. She does a sellout business in season."

Dean nodded, rubbed the back of his neck. "I guess

you'd have to call me a homebody, too. Living like I do kind of kills the old social life."

Was that his way of telling her he wasn't involved with anybody? She wondered why he'd felt the urge to reveal that.

She wished she wasn't pleased.

Dean cleared off the starboard bench and sat, patting the brown cushion next to him.

Instead, she pushed aside a stack of magazines and paperbacks and sat opposite him on the port bench. The magazine on top was folded back to show an article called "Exploring the Atlantic Seaboard." The author was Dean Kettering.

Dean rested his elbows on his knees, his hair obscuring his features. He raised a callused hand to his beard-darkened jaw and stroked it, producing a soft scraping sound that sent a buzz of sensation coursing over her.

Sighing, he said, "I don't guess I can blame you for...wanting to keep your distance. One thing you've always been good at is taking care of yourself, and I'm—" he dragged a hand through his hair "—nothing but trouble."

"Dean..."

"I understand that." He raised his gaze to hers. "I'm cool with that, but that doesn't mean you can't take the money."

"There's nothing to discuss here, Dean," she said softly. "I came here to give you back that check, and that's what I'm going to do. You can't change my mind."

"Damn it, Laura." Dean curled his hands into fists,

then spread them beseechingly. "I'm just trying to do the right thing here. Let me do the right thing for once. Please." He entreated her with his gaze; she saw his jaw clench.

Taking a deep breath, she set her coffee cup on the little table. "I can't accept your money, Dean."

"Why not?"

She looked away from the puzzlement in his eyes. "I just can't. Don't ask me to explain it."

In a low voice, he asked, "Are you that mad at me?"

"No. It's not—"

"'Cause you have a right to be." He scraped his hair back with both hands. "I mean, I can understand it if you hate me."

"I don't hate you. It's not that."

"Then why won't you take the money?"

"It..." She sat back and closed her eyes, a little whimper of frustration escaping her. "It wouldn't be right."

A heartbeat later, she felt his hands, hot and rough, wrap around hers. Startled, she opened her eyes to find him kneeling in front of her, his gaze fiercely imploring. "It'd be the most *right* thing I can think of, Laura, the most right thing I've ever done. Maybe the *only* right thing I've ever done, the only thing I didn't do for purely selfish reasons. I want you to have that money."

"I don't want it."

He raised a skeptical eyebrow. "You don't want a million dollars?"

"It's *your* money, Dean, not mine."

"I lucked into it," he said lightly. "I won't miss it."

"*How'd* you luck into it? Where did it come from?"

"It doesn't matter," he said, a little self-consciously. "It was just...someone wanted to thank me for something I did. It's not important."

"Oh, my God. It was a reward, wasn't it? For saving those two boys."

"How do you know about that?"

"The Internet."

"Yeah? I never would have pegged you for one of those propeller-heads."

"Not me." She couldn't help smiling. "My friend Kay. It was how we found you."

"Ah. Of course." Dean rubbed his thumbs over her hands. "The money doesn't mean a thing to me, Laura. I mean it when I say I won't miss it. I want you to have it."

"I..." She wrested her gaze from his and tried to pull her hands away, but his grip was too tight. "I don't need it."

He made a *tsking* sound. "The Laura I used to know could never have lied so baldly."

Laura's face grew warm, but she met his gaze squarely. "You're not the only one who can develop new bad habits."

He studied her in an astute way that penetrated right through her. "No. You still hate lying, and you can't do it worth a damn. And you sure as hell need that money. You need it and you want it."

"But I'm not going to take it."

"What about Jane?"

"What?"

"Your daughter, Jane. Even if you don't want the

money for yourself, don't you think you'd be short-changing her if—"

"I call her Janey, not Jane," Laura said. "How did you know about her?"

A telltale something stirred in his eyes, all too expressive despite his efforts to be unreadable.

"How did you know?" she repeated when he hesitated in answering. "You and I haven't seen each other in six years. How did you know I had a daughter, and what I named her?"

"I..." He shrugged, looked away—although he still held her hands in his.

"Is it too much to ask for the truth here, Dean? Am I the only person in the world who still believes in real honesty—as in telling the truth even when it isn't easy?"

A fleeting smile quirked his lips. "Probably." His expression sobered; he shifted his gaze to her hands and rubbed them between his. "You're right, though. I owe you the truth. I didn't want to tell you, 'cause I felt a little...funny about it, like a stalker or something. But a couple of years ago, I hired a private investigator to look you up, find out where you were living, how your life was going, that kind of thing."

"You're kidding. Why?"

"I just needed to make sure you were okay, you know—that things were all right for you, that you were getting along."

"Most people, if they want to check up on an old friend, do it themselves."

His eyes froze over with that inaccessible look she

loathed so much, like a door closing on his soul. "Yeah, well, I'm not like most people."

"Have you gotten to be that much of a loner that you can't even pick up the phone, or drop someone a line—"

"Laura, you *know* me," he said heatedly. "I've never been the kind of guy to 'drop someone a line.' I keep to myself 'cause whenever I don't, I just end up bringing misery down on other people. You should know that better than anyone."

Laura looked pointedly away, her cheeks burning.

"Laura." He released one of her hands to seize her chin and turn her to face him. Gentling his voice, he said, "Take the money. Take it. I want you to have it."

She shook her head.

"If you won't take it for yourself, take it for Janey."

Janey's the reason I can't take it. But she couldn't tell him that, not now, not ever. "No, Dean. I can't take it. I won't take it. I know you don't understand, but I just...I can't."

He closed his eyes briefly. When he opened them, his gaze roamed slowly over her, alighting on her eyes, her hair, her mouth. Still holding one of her hands as he knelt before her, he caressed her face, his work-roughened fingers grazing her jawline, her cheek, her temple.

Very quietly he asked, "Does Janey look like you? Or more like Will?"

"Like...like me," Laura murmured, breathlessly aware of his warmth and of his subtle, indefinable scent, still so familiar to her, and so seductive, after all these years.

"She must be beautiful, then." He threaded his fingers through her hair, curled them around the sensitive nape of her neck.

She closed her eyes, tried to steady her breathing, tried to keep from swaying toward him, astounded and appalled at how drawn she was to him still, after everything that had transpired between them.

I'm not like most people, he'd said. *I'm no pack animal.* It was true. He wasn't like her, or Will, or anyone else she'd ever known. He was her antithesis, a solitary creature who answered to no one but himself, a beast of prey who needed to go his own way, who could never be domesticated, could never learn to live in her world. Everything that meant anything to her—especially those all-important bonds of marriage and family—he held in contempt.

Dean Kettering was nothing but trouble, just as he'd said. She'd always known it, and it had always frightened her, deep down inside—frightened her, but fascinated her, too.

And, God help her, it still did.

"Does she have your eyes?" he asked.

"No." *She has yours.*

Laura felt his breath warm on her face, tickling her lips. She opened her eyes, pulled away from him, wrenched her hand from his. "I've got to go."

"Laura—"

"Let me go." Pushing him away, Laura stood and turned toward the galley. "I can't stay here."

Leaping to his feet, Dean grabbed her arm before she could pass through the doorway. "Don't do this,

Laura. You don't have to run away from me. I promise I'll leave you a—"

"Let me go, Dean," she said, struggling.

"I'll leave you alone," he said gruffly, seizing her other arm from behind. "For real. Take the money and I'll never bother you again."

She closed her eyes. All she could hear was their harsh breathing, all she could feel was his chest, rock-hard against her back, his hands like bands of iron.

"That's what you want, isn't it?" he asked, his tone resigned but laced with a hint of bitterness. "For me to be out of the picture for good?"

Why did Laura feel a pinch of contrition, when their six years of estrangement had been his doing? After that fateful night, he'd been the one to cut her out of the picture, not the other way around.

Ah, but it was so much more complicated than that. If she was contrite, it was because she felt compelled to keep the truth about Janey from him. Never mind that she had good reasons for doing so. She couldn't help but feel guilty about keeping such a secret.

And, in light of that secret, she couldn't possibly accept his money. How could she live with herself?

"Take the money," he said.

She shook her head. "It would be better for everyone—you, me...and Janey—if you'd just let me go. Please, Dean."

"Why won't you let me do this, Laura?" he asked, loosening his grip on her arms and smoothing his hands up and down them. "Just let me do this one decent thing. I know I can't undo...that night...what I did...."

"No." Laura turned to face him. "It can never be undone." In her mind's eye, she conjured up a vision of Janey in her dinosaur jammies and T-rex slippers, giggling and blowing big, silly kisses at her from Kay's front porch as she drove away early this morning. She smiled. "The truth is, I wouldn't want to undo it even if I could."

That seemed to leave him speechless.

Laura reached up with one hand and cupped his face. He closed his eyes, rubbed his prickly cheek against her palm.

"Goodbye, Dean." She stepped into the galley, put on her parka, took out the check and laid it on the counter.

In the entrance to the companionway, she looked back and saw him watching her, his hands gripping the edges of the doorway, his eyes bleak.

She turned and bolted up the stairs.

5

DEAN GRIPPED the door frame with white knuckles as he listened to her leap from the boat onto the dock and sprint away. She fled like a creature pursued who had no intention of being captured.

Releasing the door frame, he clawed his hands through his hair and let out a pent-up breath. The green envelope lay on the galley counter, scrawled on and dog-eared, a million-dollar check no one wanted tucked away inside.

No, that wasn't quite right, Dean mentally corrected himself as he lifted the envelope and brought it to his nose, inhaling the faintest whisper of her scent. She still wore the same light, grassy cologne she'd worn in college, the one that reminded him of a breeze drifting over a freshly mowed meadow. Her hair had smelled different, and still did—richly floral. The two fragrances merged to produce a paradoxical and altogether devastating bouquet of innocence and lush sensuality.

Sighing, Dean tossed the envelope back on the counter. It wasn't that nobody wanted the money. Dean wanted it himself, but in a seemingly futile stab at nobility—not his long suit—he was trying to force it on Laura. Laura wanted it, too, but for mysterious reasons of her own, she wouldn't take it.

Don't ask me to explain it....

And then, when her stonewalling had fallen on deaf ears, *I don't want it...I don't need it.* Outright lies, which he'd never thought to hear from her lips.

Laura Sweeney, lying. Or trying to. Which implied desperation.

She felt compelled to refuse the money—which she needed as much as he did, or more—but was desperate to keep the reason for her refusal a secret from him.

She'd turned downright enigmatic, his guileless little Lorelei. She'd always been so forthright, so wonderfully genuine, so plainly and simply *herself*. No pretensions, no obfuscations, no genteel white lies from Laura Sweeney.

Yet now she was hiding something, this excruciatingly honest woman who'd always worn everything right there on the surface for everybody to see. It was the only conclusion he could draw. *I can't take it...I won't take it. I know you don't understand....*

No, he didn't understand, but he damn well meant to.

Retreating to the main cabin, he fed another chunk of wood to the fire and gazed into it, sorting through the things Laura had said—and speculating on the things she'd kept to herself. Fitting pieces together, taking them apart and fitting them together differently.

It almost certainly had to do with that night. Dean braced his arms on either side of the fireplace to watch the flames leap and twitch, to feel their crackling heat infuse him, stoking his memories of that night—the night that still haunted his dreams, although reminders of it shamed him.

I wouldn't undo it even if I could.

That had stunned and perplexed him. Time and again Dean had fantasized about going back to that night and doing it right this time—resisting her, as he should have. Walking away. Being strong for both of them. Being a different kind of man, the kind of man Will had wanted him to be, expected him to be. A man of honor, a man of restraint.

He'd tried, in his own half-assed way, to do the right thing. At first.

He'd tried to leave on the sly—the coward's way out. Still, it would have worked, if she hadn't caught him.

The kiss...it had just happened. A mistake, yes, of course it was a mistake, but it had overwhelmed him, the need to kiss her. To warn her off.

To scare her. Had it?

It had scared *him*, shaken him to the core to feel her mouth hot against his, her body quivering with shock and maybe something else, something more....

But he'd tried. He'd tried. "Now do you see why I have to go?"

And then her response, softly spoken, a little shaky. "No, Dean. You don't."

The whole world shifted crazily then. Joy and terror suffused him.

Go, he commanded himself, his back to her, fists trembling at his sides. *Leave. Walk away.*

He knew she was grief stricken and lonely, didn't

know what she was saying, hadn't worked out the ramifications.

He knew, and yet he turned and came to her, grabbed her and kissed her again, just as hard as before, reckless with long-suppressed desire.

He banded his arms around her, crushing her hard to his body, moving against her in helpless need. She broke the kiss with a little indrawn breath that sounded almost like a whimper, a plea.

For one immeasurable moment their gazes met in the darkened room, lit only by what little moonlight filtered through the lace curtains. Would she push him away? he wondered, heart thundering.

She didn't, thank God. She didn't.

Framing his face with her hands, she kissed him. *She* kissed *him*.

His heart kicked. He jerked awkwardly at her robe. She lost her footing, tumbled backward onto the sleep-rumpled bed.

He fell on her, renewing the ruthless kiss as he yanked at her nightclothes. Buttons popped.

She gasped as he tore her nightgown open, filling one hand with soft, hot flesh as the other fumbled with the gown's skirt, raising it to her hips.

He couldn't see her—not well, anyway—but he could feel her, even through her bunched-up flannel nightgown. She was so warm, so womanly, and she smelled so good, and she was wet and arched her hips when he touched her.

She tried to tug his denim jacket off, but he was too impatient, wanted too much to be inside her. Still fully clothed, he unzipped his jeans and freed himself.

Her legs cradling him, she shifted her hips, positioning him right where he needed to be, where he'd ached to be for years, imagined during countless sleepless nights.

Poised for entrance, heart thudding, he hesitated briefly to savor this moment, this dizzying anticipation.

This is Laura, my Lorelei. I'm making love to Lorelei.

He could barely see her, but he could tell that her eyes were closed. And then an awful thought snaked its way through his euphoria and into his consciousness.

She's imagining I'm Will. She wishes I were him.

The thought shouldn't have devastated him—she was a recent widow, after all—but it did.

Then something miraculous happened. She whispered his name.

"Dean," she breathed, opening her eyes, those heart-stopping golden eyes, and looking right at him, her hands closing over his shoulders, her hips tilting, urging him into her.

It's me she's making love to, he realized with a burst of savage gratification. *Me, not him.*

That knowledge undid him, stripped him of his doubts and misgivings, peeled away all rational thought and left him in the realm of pure sensation, pure animal hunger.

Rearing over her, he flexed his hips and drove into her, a hard, smooth lunge that sank him deep, deep inside her, forcing a cry of fierce masculine pleasure from his throat.

Laura moaned at the abrupt joining, clawed at his

jacket, rocked against him. Her slick internal walls gripped him as he withdrew and plunged again, and again, his movements driven by brute instinct, the timeless thrill of penetration.

And something more, something he'd never felt with any of his forgettable erstwhile girlfriends—the exaltation of two people coming together as one. He felt a sense, not only of possession, but of sharing, of a physical coupling that echoed the long-standing, silent, secret communion of two hearts.

He gave himself up to his body's command, thrusting in an ever more frantic rhythm, with which she kept pace. It was a delirium of mutual pleasure, which crested swiftly, not just for him, but for her.

He felt the shuddering tension in her legs, her hips, heard a little panting cry escape her as her head fell back, something almost like panic glittering in her eyes.

Knowing she was on the edge of climax, and that he'd done this to her, that he'd made her come apart this way, filled him with triumphant satisfaction. He felt his own release gather up along with hers, their bodies straining together, trembling....

Their pleasure erupted like a single thunderclap cracking open the skies, rocking them with its power as they clutched at each other, breathless and moaning.

As the tremors diminished, he rested his weight on her, carefully, his arms tight around her, his face buried in her sweetly fragrant hair, willing his heart to quell its painful pounding. Even through his jacket, he could feel the soft weight of her breasts rising and falling.

He waited for her breathing to slow, as his was slowing, but it only grew more rapid and erratic. Presently he felt her chest begin to shake, just slightly. No sound came from her, but he realized she'd begun to weep.

"Laura?" Dean levered himself up on an elbow. She turned away from him. He felt her silent sobs deep inside her, where they were still intimately connected. "Oh, God, Laura." Easing a hand between them, Dean drew himself carefully out of her and zipped up, pulled her nightgown down, wrapped her robe around the torn garment.

She curled away from him and covered her face with her hands.

Look what he'd done to her, look what he'd reduced her to, his strong, beautiful Lorelei.

"Oh, Laura. Oh, honey." Lying behind her, Dean tucked her into his embrace, nuzzled the heavy satin of her hair. "I'm sorry. I'm so sorry. I'm entirely to blame."

She shook her head, saying something in a wet, scratchy voice that he couldn't make out—not that he needed to. The reason for her anguish was obvious. She felt as if she'd betrayed Will.

If anyone had betrayed him, it was Dean. Two months ago, William Sweeney had died in Dean's arms after pleading, with his final breath, for Dean to watch over Laura, make sure no harm ever came to her.

"I'll take care of her, buddy," Dean had managed to promise through his tears.

He'd taken care of her by seeking her out while she was holed away here licking her wounds, and...

And now *she* felt guilty?

"Don't cry, Laura, please," he said, his throat achingly full. "Don't cry. This is my fault. It was my doing. If anyone's to blame, it's me."

He held her like that for a long time, murmuring apologies and reassurances until she grew heavy and limp in his arms and he realized she'd fallen asleep. Gingerly disentangling himself from her, he slid a pillow beneath her head, pulled the quilt up over her and went downstairs.

He headed directly for the front porch, lit a cigarette with unsteady hands and leaned against a support column to smoke it.

Happy now, Kettering, you sorry son of a bitch? Hadn't screwed up in a big enough way recently, so you had to do this to Laura?

She would never forgive him. He knew that. She was compassionate and she was understanding, but she'd always valued fidelity; it was part and parcel of who she was, the whole integrity thing.

She would never forgive him for taking advantage of her while she was in mourning for Will. It didn't matter that she'd invited him to stay, with all that implied. She hadn't known what she was saying, was too dazed by the nightmare she'd endured, and was still enduring, to think straight.

It hadn't been Dean she'd wanted, not really, despite that hum of awareness between them, that aching sweetness that had always been there. It had been simple human comfort she'd craved, the most elemental kind.

Dean had known it on some level, but that hadn't stopped him. His desire for her had ambushed him, robbing him of what little he had in the way of scruples. He hadn't even had the presence of mind—the common decency—to think about protection. He had condoms in his wallet. He could have paused long enough to get one out, for her sake, but for the first time ever, it hadn't even occurred to him.

Nor, apparently, to her.

She'd been vulnerable and confused. It had been up to him to keep perspective, to keep things from getting out of hand, and he'd failed her, failed them both.

Failed Will.

Taking a last, long drag of his cigarette, Dean hurled it onto the gravel driveway and went back inside. At the foot of the stairs, he glanced through the living room, into the solarium, and saw Laura's enormous, half-finished seascape bathed in moonlight.

It was true, he thought as he crossed to the solarium for a good look at the immense canvas, with its tempestuous sky and explosive waves—that painting didn't know whether it wanted to scream or cry. It was a direct reflection of Laura's current state of mind. And that had been *before* Dean had injected himself into the mix.

I'll take care of her, buddy. Yet he'd only made things worse for Laura. What he did tonight would, if anything, intensify her grief.

He would never change, that was abundantly clear

now. Even when his intentions started out good, he couldn't help but blow it.

Turning to leave, he saw the carton he'd brought Laura sitting open amid flattened tubes of paint and spattered coffee cans on a long worktable against the wall. Curious as to whether she'd gone through it yet, he crossed to it and looked inside.

A sheet of heavy white paper, creased from being folded, lay on top of everything else. By the inadequate moonlight it looked like a drawing, but there seemed to be writing on it. He flipped a light switch on the wall above the table and blinked at the sudden onslaught of fluorescents.

It was a letter, he saw, in Laura's handwriting— "Dear Will..."—but the margins were filled with little ink drawings: Rattles, a rocking horse, little shoes, teddy bears....

Feeling suddenly starved for breath, Dean lifted the letter and read it.

Remember that night we decided to throw away my diaphragm? Talk about beginner's luck.

That's right, stallion. You hit the bull's-eye on the first try. Don't get a big head. I helped.

Yes, I'm sure it's for real. And don't try to say, you weren't doubting me, because one thing I've learned about you after all these years is that you don't believe anything unless you see the proof with your own two eyes.

I did one of those home pregnancy tests, but then, just to make sure, I went to Dr. Chang this morning. She says I'm only four or five weeks along right now, but I've got a due date! October 7—your sister Bridget's birthday.

So, what do you think? Sweating yet? Too late to take it back now, big guy. Junior and I have bonded.

Seriously, I'm shaking, I'm so happy. I wish you were here. I just wish you were here, honey, to share this with me.

Be careful over there, Will. You're a daddy now. You have a child to raise.

Listen, about names. I know we talked about it and sort of came to an agreement, but I've been thinking, and if it's a girl, I'd really like to name her Jane, after Grandma. Everyone's naming their daughters Ashley now, anyway.

Of course, if it's a boy, we're going with Dean. That hasn't changed.

Dean dropped the letter in the box, gripped the edge of the table and leaned over, squeezing his eyes shut. There was more, but he couldn't bear to read it.

Of course, if it's a boy, we're going with Dean.

Of course. Good old Dean. The prospective father's best buddy, his closest friend in the world.

And the prospective mother's...

Dean swore rawly under his breath, growling out a stream of paint-curling expletives aimed at himself.

Laura was pregnant—a good three months pregnant by now.

"You screwup, you selfish shit..." He scrubbed at his face, calling himself every loathsome name he knew.

She was carrying a child, the child of her dead husband, and Dean had...

"Oh, God."

And he hadn't been gentle about it, either. He'd waited so long to have her that, when the opportunity came, he'd just lost control.

Had he been too rough with her? Had he hurt her?

No. Laura was no silent martyr type. If he'd hurt her, she would have told him, made him stop.

Not that he hadn't hurt her, just not physically.

He hoped.

Wearily, he shut off the lights, left the solarium and climbed the stairs to the second floor. At the open door to Laura's bedroom, he paused, watching her sleep, still curled on her side like a child. A breeze fluttered the curtains, letting a wavering veil of moonlight drift into the room and sweep across the bed.

Laura's hair shimmered in the diaphanous light. Her skin had a pearly, lit-from-within quality to it.

He approached the bed slowly, his gaze riveted on her. Her mouth, with its perfectly shaped lips—luxuriant, naturally pink lips he'd never been able to stop thinking about for long—was slightly open. Those spectacular eyes were closed, of course, so he wouldn't get a last look at them.

He would never see them again.

A salty network of dried tears coursed over one wide, exquisitely molded cheekbone, dissipating near her jaw. A tendril of hair, wavy from having gotten damp, clung to the side of her face. Sitting on the edge of the bed, Dean lifted it and smoothed it off her face, carefully, so as not to wake her.

He didn't wake her, but he must have disturbed her sleep, because she mumbled something unintelligible in a raspy voice.

Dean stilled for a moment, then stroked her hair, gently, soothingly. "Shh, honey, go back to sleep."

There came a soft little grunt of acquiescence, and she didn't stir again.

He lifted the quilt over her shoulders, tucking it around her as if she were a fragile thing that needed safeguarding.

Too late for that.

He leaned over her, placed a featherlight kiss on her hair and whispered, "It's been beautiful knowing you, Lorelei."

Rising, he left the bedroom without looking back, lifted his duffel and uniform from the floor of the landing, went downstairs and drove away.

6

UNDER A BRIGHT, cold, midday sun, Laura, bearing a net bag filled with oranges, climbed onto the porch that wrapped around three sides of the Blue Mist Bed and Breakfast, gave a perfunctory rap on the front door and opened it. She and Kay hadn't stood on ceremony since the day they'd met, five years ago.

Turning in the doorway, she gestured to Janey, making her way across the snow-crusted lawn that separated the two houses, clutching a grapefruit with both mittened hands, her gaze trained on her boots as she concentrated on stepping precisely in her mother's footprints.

"Hurry up, little monkey!" Laura called. "Don't want us eating all the pancakes before you get there, do you?" Sunday brunch with Kay—and, during the summer, whoever happened to be renting rooms from her at the time—had been a ritual with them for years, just like Chick Flick Night on Thursdays.

Laura liked rituals. They made her feel secure and grounded among those she cared about, imparting a very real sense of comfort that she could use right about now. Her visit to Dean in Portsmouth two days ago had left her reeling, emotionally. A nagging remorse had scratched away at her well-being ever since, producing a malaise that resisted her heroic efforts to rise above it. Her antidepressant of choice—Hershey's Kisses with Almonds, a whole bag of them ingested at regular intervals over the past thirty-six hours—hadn't so much as made a dent.

Janey picked up her pace and followed Laura into the house. "My nose is wunning, Mommy."

"Here." Snatching a tissue from her pocket, Laura traded it for the grapefruit. "Remember—leave your boots and coat by the front door," she instructed as she kicked off her own boots. Juggling the fruit, she wrestled herself out of her parka and hung it on Kay's antique coat tree.

The mingled aromas of bacon, coffee and hot buttermilk pancakes drifting through the house made Laura's stomach gripe emptily. All she'd had to eat that morning was half a container of vanilla yogurt on her way out the door to church.

"Meet you in the kitchen." Mouth watering, Laura padded in her stocking feet past the front parlor and oak-banistered stairway, through the dining room with its economy-size table set for four—*four?*—and into the spacious, sun-washed kitchen with its teacup wallpaper and eyelet curtains.

"Laura!" Kay, standing at the massive industrial stove cooking pancakes, turned to her friend with a peculiar, strained smile. "You're here!" Turning back to the stove, she asked, a little too brightly, "Where's Janey?"

"She's coming."

"Good. Good."

Laura thunked the oranges and grapefruit on the

tiled countertop. "Kay, how come the table's set for four?"

"What?" Kay flipped a pancake, but without her usual skill; it landed partly off the griddle, but she didn't seem to notice.

"There are four place settings on the dining table, not three. Is someone else—"

"Oh, hey, listen, you should get that fruit cut up. The bacon's done, and the pancakes are almost there."

"Uh..." Laura reached for the wooden cutting board. "Is something wrong, Kay?"

"What do you mean?" Kay asked without looking at her.

"I mean you're acting a little...crisped around the edges."

"No, I'm not."

"Yes you are."

"I'm just dying of hunger, that's all. How was church?"

"How was *church*?" Laura chuckled disbelievingly as she lifted Kay's biggest knife off its hook, placed the grapefruit in the middle of the chopping board and sliced it in half, releasing its tart-sweet perfume. "Now I *know* something's up." The one time Laura had managed to bully her friend into coming to church with her, Kay had fled midway through the service with "the worst fake migraine I've ever had."

"What do you mean?" Kay flipped a couple more pancakes, none too adeptly. "Just 'cause I've got issues with organized religion doesn't mean I can't show an interest."

"Well, at least you didn't call it 'organized superstition' this time." Setting the grapefruit halves on the big, cut glass platter they used for fruit, Laura started whacking the oranges into wedges. Janey turned her nose up at grapefruit, but she could put away oranges like a machine.

"Mmm, smells yummy in here!" Janey exclaimed as she entered the kitchen.

"Hey, monkey," Laura called over her shoulder as she chopped. "What took you so long?"

"I was talkin' to Dean Kettle-wing."

Laura's knife stilled in midslice. Her gaze shot to Kay, who met it sheepishly. "Laura, I, uh..."

"Morning, Kay," came a man's voice—Dean's voice—from behind her, and then, more softly, "Laura."

Laura felt as if her chest were being crushed in a vise. Yanking the knife out of the orange, she turned to find Dean standing in the doorway to the kitchen.

Next to Janey.

Dean and Janey together. They'd been *talking.* Laura struggled just to draw a breath.

Dean, dressed in an age-softened Henley shirt and jeans, his hair pulled back into a ponytail, squatted on his haunches and stage-whispered to Janey, "She doesn't look happy to see me."

"You just think that 'cause she's pointing a big knife at you," Janey whispered back, "but I don't think she knows she's doing it."

Kay pried the knife out of Laura's hand, set it on the counter and grinned like a lunatic. "Everyone hungry?"

"Dean," Laura said woodenly, "what the hell are you doing here?"

Janey slapped a hand over her mouth in reaction to the "hell," and possibly also to the depth of Laura's ire; she had rarely seen her phlegmatic mother angry, and never seen her rude.

Piling the last of the pancakes on an already heaping platter, Kay said, "He, uh, he showed up yesterday evening and asked if I rented out rooms during the winter. I said not usually, but only 'cause there's so little demand. I gave him a special off-season weekly rate and put him in the Sage Room 'cause it's got the firepl—"

"I asked *him*." Laura took a step toward Dean, who rose to his feet with that shuttered expression she knew all too well. "What are you *doing* here?"

When Dean hesitated, Janey jumped in. "Mommy, this is the man that gave you the million—"

"I know who he is," Laura said shortly. "Janey, it was Mr. Kettering I went to see over the weekend. I gave the money back."

Janey looked stricken. "You gave it *back*? But what about Mr. Hale's boat?"

"Janey, please," Laura said. "I'm trying to talk to—"

"We can talk while we eat," Kay inserted too cheerily as she handed the platter of pancakes to Dean. "Would you mind putting those on the dining table? I'll get the coffee and bacon. Janey, you grab the juice—you know where it is, right?"

"Yup!" Janey scampered over to the big steel refrigerator and hauled it open with both hands.

"And, Laura, if you'll bring the fruit out—"

"I'm going to kill you for this," Laura muttered between her teeth as Kay passed by her.

"Fair enough, but can we eat first? I really am starving."

"WHAT'S THIS ABOUT A BOAT?" Dean asked as he mopped up a puddle of syrup with his last bite of pancake. Kay had seated him directly across from Laura, forcing her to make eye contact with him at regular intervals all through brunch—except when she had studiously avoided doing so. No one seemed to have noticed Laura's almost complete silence during the meal. Even the taciturn Dean had contributed more to the conversation than she had.

Kay said, "There's a used sailboat Laura's got her eye on."

"It's a Pwecision 18!" exclaimed Janey, perched on a stack of phone books at the head of the table. "Waleigh Hale is selling it. It's five years old, just like me. Only Mommy says we can't afford it."

Laura sighed as she lifted her coffee cup.

"A Precision 18," Dean said. "Nice boat. How much is this Wally Hale asking?"

Laura choked on her coffee at the notion of such a venerable old personage being mislabeled "Wally." "It's *Raleigh* Hale," she said through a chuckle she couldn't suppress. "His family founded Hale's Point, a couple of towns over."

Dean caught her eye and said softly, "It's nice to see you smile."

Laura looked away quickly and caught Kay eyeing

her with a smile that said *verrry interesting*. Partly to undercut whatever revelation Kay had come to, Laura added an edge to her voice and said to Dean, "Look, I don't know where this is going, but it doesn't really matter how much Raleigh is asking for the boat, because—"

"Eighty-seven hundwed," Janey said. "Mommy says we could fix the porch and the woof and about a hundwed other things with that kind of money—if we had it."

"What a tragedy to have to make that choice," Dean said.

"Not having food to eat or a roof over our heads would be a tragedy," Laura corrected. "Not having a sailboat I can live with."

"But why should you have to?"

"Now it comes." Laura sat back, crossing her arms. "This is why you came here, isn't it? To try and force me into taking that money."

"No."

Laura regarded him dubiously.

"You told me you wouldn't take it." Dean calmly drained his orange juice. "I believe you."

Janey and Kay, who had brightened at the prospect of his forcing her to take the money, both seemed to deflate just a little.

"Then what are you doing here?" Laura asked.

He shrugged his big shoulders. "To tell you the truth, it does get just a little claustrophobic, spending all winter in that boat. During your visit the other day..." His mouth quirked. "I'm sorry, can I call it that? I know you hadn't intended it to be a *visit*."

Laura glared at him.

"Anyway," Dean continued with a mild smile, "you mentioned this friend of yours who'd turned the old Sullivan Place into a B and B called the Blue Mist. I kinda liked the name. It's...I don't know. Evocative. Inviting."

Kay perked up. "Yeah?"

"Oh, please," Laura muttered into her coffee.

"So I arranged for someone to take care of the *Lorelei*," Dean said, "and rented a Jeep and drove on down."

"Any idea how long you'll be staying?" Kay asked as she reached behind her for the vitamin chest she kept on the sideboard.

"I'm not much for plans and schedules." Leaning back in his chair with his coffee cup, Dean said, "A few weeks, maybe longer."

"*Longer?*" Laura exclaimed.

"I don't really have to be back in Portsmouth till the end of May, when it's time to set off for Bermuda. That gives me a couple of months to burn off any old way I want." Setting his coffee cup down, Dean pulled his cigarettes from the back pocket of his jeans and shook one out.

Janey actually gasped. "You smoke cigawettes?"

"Not in my B and B, he doesn't," Kay proclaimed as she sorted through the tablets and capsules in her vitamin chest, plucking some out to add to a little parti-colored heap beside her juice glass. "Sorry, Dean, but the Blue Mist is a stink-free zone. You'll have to take it outside."

"You shouldn't smoke." Janey eyed the rumpled

pack of Marlboros as if it were a rusty hypodermic filled with heroin. Laura realized this might be the first time her daughter had ever seen a pack of cigarettes, since they didn't know anyone else who smoked. "Smoking is bad for you. Mrs. Doyle said cigawettes kill people."

"Mrs. Doyle is her teacher at preschool," Laura explained. "Janey, finish your juice—remember what I said about drinking what you pour. And don't be lecturing grown-ups about what they do."

"No, that's okay," Dean said as he pocketed the cigarettes. "I can take it. Mrs. Doyle is right, Janey. Smoking is a terrible habit."

"Then why do you do it?" Janey asked in seemingly genuine bewilderment.

Dean emitted a cross between a sigh and a chuckle. "I've been smoking since I was thirteen. When you've been doing a certain thing for a long time, it can be hard to stop."

"I know." Janey nodded sympathetically. "I sucked my thumb ever since I was a baby. But it was making my teeth come in cwooked, so I had to stop. It dwove me cwazy! But after a while it got better, and now I never even want to put my thumb in my mouth." She frowned thoughtfully. "Almost never."

"That's very admirable," Dean praised. "I'm proud of you."

"You could quit smoking," Janey said. "And then I could be pwoud of *you!*"

"If only it were that easy." Dean rubbed his cleanly-shaved jaw. "I've been smoking most of my life."

"I sucked my thumb *all* of my life! Even when I was in Mommy's tummy—she saw it on the ultwasound!"

"She's got you there." Grinning, Kay tossed a handful of pills in her mouth and washed them down with a swallow of orange juice.

"You should twy to quit," Janey counseled solemnly. "Just *twy* it. Take it a day at a time," she added, echoing Laura's advice to her when it was time for her little twelve-step lose-the-thumb program.

Dean laughed softly, looking years younger than he had when Laura had confronted him in Portsmouth Friday. "All right. I'll try."

"Weally?"

"Weally. Now, finish your juice."

"So, Dean." Kay snapped her vitamin chest shut. "Were you serious when you said that about staying here till the end of May?"

"Yep." Dean reached for his coffee cup.

"You're going to stay here for *two months*?" Laura asked.

"Maybe." Dean took a slow sip of coffee, his gaze trained on Laura. "Is that a problem?"

Laura's gaze snapped automatically to Janey; her stomach clenched. Pushing her chair back, she said, "Dean, can I talk to you alone?"

After a moment's hesitation, Dean lowered his coffee cup and rose. "Sure. How about a walk on the beach?"

"DEAN, WHY DID YOU come here?" Laura asked when they were about a hundred yards down the beach, which was flecked with patches of snow that became sparser near the erupting waves.

"Haven't you already asked me that, like, a dozen times?" Dean glanced at her as they walked. She'd donned sunglasses in addition to that big green parka of hers and those utilitarian duck boots, so he couldn't see her eyes.

"Every time I ask it," she said, looking straight ahead, her gloved hands jammed in the pockets of her parka, "you either put me off or feed me a line of bull."

"When did I—"

"You know and I know you didn't come all the way down here—to stay for *two months*—"

"Maybe."

"—because you like the name of Kay's B and B. You've got an agenda."

"Me? An agenda?"

"Dean, just please—"

"She's great," he said.

Laura exhaled a giant cloud of vapor. "You're changing the subject."

"My newest bad habit, like I said. She is, though—she's a hoot."

Turning to look at Dean, Laura said, "That's why Kay and I became such good friends, I think. She's so—"

"Not Kay. Janey."

Laura looked abruptly away from him, staring straight ahead. He couldn't make out her expression because of those damned shades.

"She's a live one." Dean paused, yanking off his

right glove to extract his cigarettes from his back jeans pocket. "Stubborn and opinionated, just like her old man."

Laura stopped walking as well, and turned to confront him, hands on hips. "What are you doing?"

"Uh...lighting a cigarette?"

"Didn't you just tell Janey you were going to quit?"

A little huff of laughter rose in Dean's throat. "Yeah, well, you know...that was..."

"Was what? A lie?"

He wished he could see her eyes. Was she actually ticked off at him? "I told her I'd quit to...you know...be polite."

"You mean to placate her. You lied to shut her up."

"Come on, Laura. Be real."

"I don't like having my child lied to. About anything. Nothing could be more real."

Reaching out, Dean plucked Laura's sunglasses off before she could stop him. Her eyes were fiercely gold in the early afternoon sun.

"You're serious," he said quietly. "I should have known. You've always been such a nut for honesty."

For some reason Laura's cheeks, already ruddy from the cold, grew even pinker.

"All right, you've shamed me into it. Here." Dean handed her his cigarettes. "Do me a favor and flush those, okay?"

"Really?" She looked down at the crumpled pack of Marlboros and back up at him. "You're really quitting?"

He smiled. "I wouldn't want to be guilty of deceiving an innocent child."

Shoving the pack in a pocket of her parka, Laura asked, "So, why did you come here? I'm going to keep asking till I get a credible answer."

Pulling his glove back on, Dean said, "Why did you come to Portsmouth two days ago?"

Laura regarded him in silence for a few seconds, the color in her cheeks deepening even further. *Interesting...* Averting her gaze, she said, "I went to Portsmouth to return your money." She held out her hand. "Can I have my sunglasses back?"

"No. Not yet." He knew why she wanted them back. She was trying to shield her thoughts and feelings from him, to conceal whatever it was she was hiding from him, as contrary to her nature as such deception might be.

She crossed her arms, her jaw set, bronzed tendrils of hair dancing in the breeze off the ocean. "What are you going to do with the money, now that I won't take it?"

"Put it in the bank, I guess."

"Then what?" she asked, her voice tinged with suspicion.

He turned her sunglasses over in his hands, catching his own smiling reflection in the green-tinted lenses.

"You're planning something," she said.

"Me? Make plans?" He slid her sunglasses on over his own eyes and adjusted them. "I'm a creature of impulse, remember? I do whatever moves me at the moment."

She reached up and grabbed the glasses off him. "How could I forget?"

As she was about to put the glasses back on, he clamped a hand around her wrist. "You don't always tell the truth. You said Janey had Will's eyes."

"I never said that."

"You said she didn't have yours. Which would imply that she has Will's. Only she doesn't."

Laura stared at him unblinkingly as he lifted her chin, the better to study those astonishing eyes—amber imbedded with flecks of gold leaf.

"No one in the world has eyes like these," he murmured. "No one but you."

He wanted to kiss her. He ached to kiss her. She lured him as the moon lured the tides; she always had, always would.

I'll leave you alone, he'd told her in Portsmouth. *Take the money and I'll never bother you again.*

But she hadn't taken the money, wouldn't take it. By rights he should feel no compunction about acting on the irresistible force of nature that drew them together.

And it *was* irresistible. Six years ago, when he drove away from here in the middle of the night, he'd resolved, for her sake, never to contact her again. But he'd violated that resolution by sending her the money, and then...

The moment he'd seen her standing on that dock, shivering with the cold and maybe something else, he'd felt it again, the old longing, the hunger for her that would never be sated. He'd never wanted anything or anyone as much as he wanted Laura, had always wanted her, would always want her. He ached with it, right down to his bones.

What would she do if he took her in his arms, lowered his mouth to hers?

Dean bent his head just slightly, his gaze on her mouth, those exquisitely formed lips that always looked berry stained even without lipstick. They would feel hot against his, and soft.

She hitched in a breath, something like panic glittering in her eyes—although she made no move to pull back; she just stared at him, like a lamb facing the ax.

Through an effort of will, Dean drew away from her, released her wrist. Taking the sunglasses out of her hand, he opened them and slid them over her eyes. She was freaked out enough simply by the fact that he'd shown up here so unexpectedly. Even he knew when to lay off.

"Want to head back?" he asked.

She nodded.

Best to let her get used to his being around, he reflected as they walked in silence back to Kay's place. Laura was wary of him, frightened even—understandable in light of what had transpired the last time they were together.

Pouncing on her would only make her more apprehensive, more guarded. The way to get her to lower her defenses was to take his time, make her trust him, keep his distance.

For now. Dean didn't kid himself into thinking he could keep away from her forever. Sooner or later, his yearning for her would get to be too much, and he would act on it. Which would, of course, be a monumental mistake.

Not that that had ever stopped him before.

7

"BY THE WAY," Laura told Kay the next morning as she squeezed a dab of zinc white onto the big enameled butcher tray that served as her palette, "don't think for a minute that I've forgiven you for springing Dean on me yesterday."

"I didn't *spring* him on you. Not on purpose, anyway." Kay refilled both of their mugs from the paint-spattered coffeemaker nestled among the various jars, cans and tubes on the worktable in Laura's studio, stirring just the right amount of sugar and powdered creamer into Laura's. "I rented him a room. So sue me."

"Sue you? I'm gonna kill you, remember?" Working just a touch of alizarin crimson into the white with her palette knife, Laura yelled, "Janey! Are you almost ready? You've got—" she consulted her watch, which said it was twenty to nine "—ten minutes till you have to leave. You don't want to be late today—you've got the field trip to the firehouse." And Mrs. Doyle had made a special point of begging Laura to get Janey there on time today, because they were supposed to leave at nine sharp. If Janey was late, as she often was, it would hold everybody up and throw them off schedule for the whole morning.

"I'm weady!" Janey's voice came from the direction of the living room. "I'm tyin' my sneakers."

"You were tying your sneakers five minutes ago. Are your teeth brushed?"

There was a telltale silence.

"Did you at least comb your hair and wash your face?"

"I'll do it now."

"This is all your fault," Laura muttered to Kay, who had suggested that Janey might become more self-sufficient if Laura didn't hover quite so closely while she was getting ready in the mornings. Only problem was, it now took Janey about three times longer to get out of the house than it used to when Laura had followed her around, guiding her every step of the way.

"Patience." Kay settled with a contented sigh into the tattered old easy chair Laura kept in a corner of the studio for breaks. "It takes time to develop good habits. You'll thank me later."

"Get those shoes tied *now*," Laura called out in her most commanding bellow, "and then go up to the bathroom, where you will brush your teeth, wash your face and comb your hair—*fast fast fast*—or Aunt Kay will leave without you!" She gulped down some coffee and said to Kay, "Listen, thanks for offering to drop her off on your way to the library."

"No problem. I know how it is when you're really cooking on a painting. Taking time out breaks the spell."

They both turned to look at Laura's current project, propped on an easel—a large, just-begun painting of Janey, which she'd been working on since five that morning. It was based on drawings Laura had made a couple of weeks ago after Janey had fallen asleep on the living room couch in her dinosaur jammies, clutching her raggedy stuffed stegosaurus, arms and legs at preposterous but oddly endearing angles. Laura had gotten a lot accomplished in just four hours, sketching the composition onto the primed canvas in airy brush strokes and blocking in most of the colors. The alizarin crimson was for Janey's cheeks, which blossomed with hot color when she slept.

Laura heard the stairs creak swiftly under Janey's sneakered feet, followed by the groaning of anti-quated plumbing as the child turned on the water in the bathroom sink. *Good girl*, Laura thought, although considering how long it could take her daughter to wash her face, brush her teeth and comb her hair, it was still doubtful that she'd be ready in—Laura gave her watch another quick glance—eight minutes.

Turning back to her worktable, she dipped the tip of her palette knife into a baby food jar she'd filled with linseed oil, and added two drops to the pale pink she'd concocted. Kneading the oil into the pigment, she said, "I just about stroked out when I saw Dean standing there next to Janey in your kitchen yesterday. I can't believe you went ahead and rented him a room just like that. Why didn't you call me?"

"Because you would have told me to turn him away."

"Damn straight."

"I figured it'd be easier to go ahead and rent him the room and incur your wrath than to try and talk you into okaying it, which you wouldn't have, but I would have done it anyway, and you would have ended up even more aggravated."

"You know, Kay, you really are a world-class pain in the butt sometimes."

"You love me, anyway," Kay said smugly.

"Except when I hate you." Laura grabbed a paint-smeared coffee can full of turpentine, stuck her palette knife into it and dripped a bit of its contents into the crimson-cheeked pink. From somewhere outside came a dull *thwack*, and then another, and another, which conjured up a mental picture of Lizzie Borden executing her own unique brand of pain-in-the-butt control.

"A penny for your thoughts," Kay ventured with feigned timidity.

"I'm thinking it's a shame the ground's too frozen to bury a body right now, or I might be tempted to give that shiny new ax of mine quite a workout."

"Yeah, well...I think it's getting enough of a work-out already." Kay nodded toward the floor-to-ceiling mullioned windows that formed the south wall of Laura's solarium turned studio.

Pivoting, Laura followed Kay's line of sight, squinting at the sun reflecting off the icy patches of partially melted snow in the side yard. The cordwood she'd had delivered last week rose in a disorderly heap higher than a tall man—higher, at any rate, than the tall man who now hefted a sizable chunk of oak off of it one-handed, the other being wrapped around the handle of Laura's ax.

Dean. Laura spat out the sort of epithet she would

never in a million years want Janey to hear coming out of her mouth.

Dean's hair was unbound this morning, and fluttered in the chilly breeze off the Sound as he turned his back to them, slammed the chunk of wood onto the chopping block and raised the ax. He had on the same blue Shetland sweater and raggedy scarf he'd been wearing in Portsmouth the other day. Now, as then, his sleeves were pushed up, displaying forearms cabled with muscle. The sweater looked worn and hung slackly on him, except across the solid breadth of his shoulders, which bulged and shifted as he brought the ax down with a crack.

Kay chuckled throatily, then took a sip of coffee. "The view outside that window just got a *whole* lot prettier."

"What is he doing?" Laura asked dully.

"Uh...chopping up your cordwood?"

"*Why?*"

"Because it's a job you hate and he likes to stay busy. Keeps his mind off cigarettes. Least that's what he told me this morning."

Laura turned to look at Kay. "You knew he was going to come over here and do this and you didn't warn me?"

Kay's eyes widened with poorly feigned mystification. "I didn't *warn* you that he's planning on doing you this monumental favor?"

"You know what I mean," Laura accused, wagging the palette knife at Kay. "You *know* I don't want to have anything to do with that man!"

"All I know is he's got you so worked up that

within the past twenty-four hours you've threatened me, your best friend in the world, with a knife, an ax, and now a...whatever the heck that thing is called."

Laura hurled the palette knife across the room to the accompaniment of another blistering curse.

"I take it back," Kay said with that shrewd little smile of hers. "That's not all I know."

"What do you mean?"

"I mean I'm not stupid. I may have tanked on my math SATs, but I've still got enough fingers to add and subtract, as long as the answer isn't higher than ten. And the number of months between April 2, 1995, when Dean came to visit you here, and the following January 1, when Janey was born, is..."

Oh, God. Laura leaned back against her worktable, feeling suddenly weak, as Kay made a show of counting off the months on her fingers.

"...six, seven, eight..." Kay looked up, wriggling her right ring finger. "Why, what do you know? It was exactly nine...oh. Oh, honey, I'm sorry."

Laura must have looked utterly stricken, because Kay bolted out of her chair, instantly serious, and put her arms around her. "I'm sorry, Laura. I'm an ass. I shouldn't have been so flip. This must be anything but funny to you."

"When did you figure it out?" Laura asked hollowly.

"Last night. You'd never told me exactly when Will died—I guess I'd always assumed it was late spring or in the summer. I was lying in bed thinking about what you said, about Dean coming here that April, two months after Will died. So I...I don't know. The lightbulb just went off, and..."

Laura groaned and covered her face with her hands. *Stupid, stupid, stupid, stupid.* She'd been so rattled the other day by that check and the fact that Dean had sent it that she'd slipped up royally, without even realizing it! *Stupid!*

"Does anyone else know?" Kay asked. "I mean, that Will wasn't...wasn't Janey's..."

Laura shook her head. "Even Grandma Jane never found out, although she would have if she'd lived long enough. See, I'd miscarried Will's baby in February, right after he died, so—"

"Oh, Laura." Kay hugged her. "I'm really sorry."

"So she would have known Will couldn't have been the father this time. But she died that summer before I'd worked up the nerve to tell her. I wasn't even showing yet."

"No one else did the math?" Kay asked disbelievingly.

"I've got hardly any relatives—neither did Will—and I never see them. I'm out of touch with all my old friends, except for Christmas cards and the like. People know about Janey, but they all assume she's Will's."

Kay chewed her lip. "Whose name did you put on the birth certificate under 'Father'?"

Laura closed her eyes and rubbed her forehead. "I left it blank, 'cause in this state you can't name anyone without his knowledge and permission. And I just couldn't put Will's name there. He'd been dead for eleven months by that point. I just...I just couldn't lie so *baldly.*"

"You know," Kay said with a rueful little chuckle as she squeezed Laura's shoulder, "this unrelenting honesty can't be a good thing. Not in the long run."

Laura smiled in spite of the circumstances. Quietly she said, "Kay, I...I know I don't have to spell this out, but..."

Kay pulled an imaginary zipper across her lips.

Laura sagged against her. "Thanks. I just don't want any complications in Janey's life."

"Speaking of complications..." Kay nodded toward the wall of windows. Outside, Dean was working his way steadily through the pile of cordwood, reducing it into manageable pieces, which he stacked neatly against Laura's toolshed. "I take it he's got no idea he's Janey's father."

Hearing it said out loud like that—"Janey's father"—made Laura's stomach tighten. "No—thank God."

Kay slanted a look of reproach toward Laura. "For an honesty freak, you sure know how to tell a whopper when it suits you."

Her hackles rising, Laura crossed the room to pick up the palette knife she'd thrown. "I never *told* Dean that Will was Janey's father—not in so many words. He just assumed—"

"A lie of omission is still a lie, kiddo. People who pride themselves on truthfulness are supposed to know that."

"Kay, please don't lecture me," Laura said testily. "You have no idea what I went through, what I'm still going through. And if you think this is easy for me—keeping this secret—then you don't know me as well as you think you do."

Nodding thoughtfully, Kay perched on an arm of the easy chair, cradling her mug of coffee in her hands. "You're right. I've got no business making judgments. I should be trying to understand, not censure."

"That's right," Laura mumbled sullenly as she returned to her worktable.

"So, help me to understand," Kay said quietly. "Tell me what happened. You and Dean...had this been going on while you were married to Will?"

"*No!*" Laura exclaimed as heat flooded her face. "Of course not! How could you think that?"

"I didn't think it," Kay soothed, "I was just wondering. Things happen...you know, things people don't plan. Repressed desires and all that."

Expelling a ragged sigh, Laura plucked a flat bristle brush out of its can and charged it with the alizarin tint. "Yeah, well, there were repressed desires, all right, all through college, but we didn't do anything about them—we didn't even acknowledge them. I loved Will. Dean knew that." Turning, she brushed a warm flush onto Janey's deliciously fat cheeks. The effect was pretty, but the color wasn't quite deep enough.

"So that day in April when Dean came here to bring you Will's effects, that was the first time..."

Laura nodded. "The first and only. It was..." She closed her eyes and felt it again, the heat, the inevitability, her desperate need for him stripping away all sense, all misgivings...and then—*oh, yes*—the exhilarating shock of him on top of her, inside her...

But then afterward came a different kind of shock, when she realized that they had actually done it, done what they'd longed to do for years, but always had the sense to avoid...because of Will.

Will...

No sooner had Dean withdrawn from her than he'd begun apologizing. Laura's last memory of that night was weeping as he held her, whispering a litany of contrition. *This is my fault. It was my doing. If anyone's to blame, it's me.*

Knowing how deeply he regretted making love to her had only compounded Laura's anguish. After all those years of aching for each other in such ardent silence, their coming together should have been unreservedly joyous. It should have left them fulfilled, transformed. Instead, it had left them—or Laura, at any rate—consumed by guilt.

Will...

It was wrong. It must have been wrong. Will had only been gone for two months, and she'd loved him. Being with Dean that way, letting that happen...it was shameful.

But it was the next morning that cold reality had really set in.

"When I woke up," Laura said in a raw voice she barely recognized, "he was gone."

"Gone. Just...gone? No note, no—"

"He doesn't leave notes. He doesn't break things off with women. He..." Laura unscrewed the tube of alizarin crimson and squeezed some more into the patch of pink on the butcher tray. "He hates being tied down, having to answer to anybody. He's always been that way."

"Is that why he left, do you think?" Kay asked. "Because he thought you would tie him down? Or was it guilt?"

Laura nodded as she mixed the paint with her palette knife. "He probably did feel some measure of guilt, and I'm sure that didn't help, but given his history with women, and that loner thing he's got going...I'm guessing he was afraid I'd become too attached to him. All those years of lusting in my heart, and then we finally..." She swore under her breath.

"Maybe he was afraid *he'd* get too attached," Kay ventured. "Or maybe he already *felt* too attached, and he was all conflicted and—"

"You don't know Dean." Grimacing, Laura scooped up some of the new, darker crimson tint with her brush. "He doesn't get conflicted, not over women. And he sure doesn't get attached. Dean Kettering has never needed anybody but Dean Kettering, not then, not now."

As Laura turned around, she noticed Dean outside, pausing to wipe the back of his arm across his forehead, then raking a hand through his sweat-dampened hair. Wresting her gaze from him, she started deepening the color on Janey's cheeks. "He left because he decided it would be too messy if he stayed. I don't know. Maybe he was right."

"You don't believe that."

"Dean knew me, Kay. He knew how I was, how I am—a one-man woman, born to keep a house and raise kids. He used to tease me about being 'the salt of the earth.' And he used to argue with me about sex, about how it was really just about animal gratification, and how monogamy was unnatural and marriage was an institution dreamed up by women to keep men under con—"

"Yeah, yeah, yeah." Kay waved a dismissive hand. "The college boy's credo. So, you're saying he thought you'd get hung up on him if he stuck around?"

"Yep." A flash of movement from outside the windows snagged Laura's attention—Dean imbedding the ax blade into the chopping block with one swift flick of his arm before yanking the blue sweater over his head. Balling it up, he tossed it onto the stack of newly chopped wood. Beneath it he wore the old Henley shirt he'd had on yesterday, the bottom of which he pulled up to blot his face, revealing a flat abdomen ridged with muscle. "He was right," Laura said softly. "I would have gotten hung up on him. I already was."

And, God help me, I always will be.

"What did you do when you found out you were pregnant?" Kay asked.

"I cried," Laura said as she carefully brushed the darker pink onto Janey's cheeks. "Just once, but it was a pull-out-all-the-stops bawl-fest. I mean, I'd always wanted children, but the circumstances couldn't have been more screwed up. But then...I don't know, maybe it was the pregnancy hormones or something, the endorphins and all that...I calmed down and just accepted it. I had a baby inside me. It may not have been the right guy who put her there, but that didn't mean I didn't want her."

Kay nodded. "Somehow I couldn't see you wallowing in your misery for very long. You're not made that way."

"The only fly in the ointment was having to tell Grandma Jane, but of course she passed away before I got around to it, and left me this house, and a little money, which was a lifesaver. Not having a mortgage meant I didn't have to hold down a day job while I got my art career off the ground. And painting helped to keep me sane, so..." She shrugged.

"And you never considered contacting Dean and telling him about the baby?"

"Actually, I did, in the beginning. I thought he had a right to know, so I tried to locate him through the air force, but they wouldn't disclose his whereabouts. I kept thinking he'd get in touch with me, but..." She sighed heavily. "He never did."

"Ah." Kay was finally getting it, it seemed.

"He'd obviously washed his hands of me," Laura said. "It was around the time you moved here, when I was almost due, that I finally gave up on trying to find Dean. I decided my baby would be better off with no father than with one who didn't want anything to do with us. She deserved better—we both did."

"Maybe you should have tried harder to find him," Kay suggested. "Maybe he *would* have wanted something to do with you if he'd known about the baby. Maybe he even would have done the right thing and married you."

Laura spun around to face her friend. "Let's say he did, as contrary to his nature as that would have been. You can't tell me he would have stuck around for the long haul—not Dean Kettering." *I always hated toeing the line, always had an itch to go off and do my thing, regardless of how it affected anyone else.* "And a father who tosses his family aside like trash is worse than no father at all because of the scars he leaves on his kids. Dean himself is evidence of that."

"And that's why you're still refusing to tell him," Kay asked, "even though he's reestablished contact?"

"Yes, and that's why I can't take his money." Returning her attention to the painting, Laura scowled at the dark pink blotches on Janey's cheeks. "Yikes, she looks like a clown—what was I thinking?" Grabbing her palette knife, she started scraping off the paint she had so painstakingly applied. "How could I possibly take a million dollars from him while keeping a secret like this? And if I told him, it would open up a horrendous can of worms. He'd be in the picture then, he'd be Janey's father."

"Uh...he's already Janey's father," Kay pointed out evenly.

"You know what I mean. He'd be a father *figure*. He'd be important to her. And then he'd split and pull the rug out from under her, and I'd be left to pick up the pieces. No, thank you."

"Maybe you're not giving him enough credit. All things considered, he actually seems like a pretty nice guy."

"A pretty *dangerous* guy is what he is." Laura ceased her scraping and stared in dismay at the wounded-looking mess she'd made of Janey's face. Shifting her gaze, she looked outside to where Dean was methodically splitting hunk after hunk of wood, his body moving with that potent masculine grace that had always made her shiver deep in her belly.

"Well..." Kay began, "he may be a tad on the untamed side, a little reckless, a little impulsive, a bit too self-sufficient for your taste. That doesn't mean he's dangerous."

"To me it does." Moistening a rag with turp, Laura blotted up as much of the remaining crimson disaster as she could.

"That's it, isn't it?" Kay said in that all-too-knowing way of hers. "Your problem is you kinda *dig* that bad-boy thing."

"*Excuse me*? I'm into stability and commitment, remember?"

"And bad boys—or, at least, a certain bad boy. Not on a conscious level, of course. You *think* you want some nice, sweet, honorable *Father Knows Best* type who likes his hedge trimmer, his steady paycheck and the easy listening station, and on a certain level you do. But on another level—" Kay's voice lowered suggestively "—in that deeply buried place where a woman's secret drives and desires lurk..." She cocked her head toward the wall of windows. "You want to rock and roll."

With a roll of her eyes, Laura flung the rag into the trash can she reserved for flammables, and wiped her hands on the paint-crusted denim bib apron she wore over her gesso-flecked jeans and sweatshirt. Charging her brush with some flesh-toned paint, she set about covering up the faint crimson stain left on Janey's cheeks. "You know, for a shrink who supposedly doesn't believe in that stuff anymore, you sure seem to like spouting those psychological insights."

"That was just an observation," Kay corrected. "If it's insight you want, how about this. The reason you regard Dean as dangerous—and therefore won't take his money or tell him the truth about Janey, despite your honesty fetish—is because you secretly fear your overwhelming attraction to him. You're afraid that if he reciprocated your feelings, you'd throw your lot in with him—"

"And end up sorrier than I can imagine," Laura said soberly. "Especially if Janey is left traumatized because I was stupid and selfish enough to let him into our lives. Which, incidentally, isn't quite as simple as you seem to think. What am I supposed to tell Janey about Dean? 'Hey, by the way, your father wasn't my husband after all, but his best friend. Just thought you should know.'"

"She *should* know."

"You've *got* to be kidding. Trust me, Janey's a lot better off thinking—" Laura gasped. *Janey!* She'd gotten so involved in their conversation that she'd forgotten about preschool. Glancing at her watch, she groaned. "Omigod, it's almost nine o'clock. She's gonna be late for the field trip."

Tossing the brush aside, she sprinted out of the studio, down the hall and up the stairs, yelling, "Janey! Are you ready?" She flung open the bathroom door. "Janey, it's time to go. You're gonna be..." Laura blinked at her daughter, standing on her little wooden step stool, her sleeves pushed up, her arms submerged up to the elbows in a sinkful of soapy water.

Janey's unruly corn-silk mane had clearly not been combed, nor her face washed, if her dried-milk mustache was any indication. "Janey, what are you doing?"

"Washing my button collection." Janey scooped a double handful of glistening wet buttons out of water and held them up proudly.

With a frantic little growl, Laura grabbed her hairbrush off its shelf and yanked it through her daughter's tangled curls. "Take that towel off the rod and dry off."

"But my buttons are all—"

"*Now!*"

"Ow!" Janey whined as she grudgingly dried her hands and arms. "You're bwushing too—"

Tossing the brush aside, Laura dipped a corner of the towel in the sink and used it to perform a quick 'n' dirty cleanup of Janey's face. The teeth would just have to go unbrushed. "You were supposed to be getting ready! Now you'll be late for the field trip."

"Can I just dwy my buttons off?" Janey asked plaintively as Laura hustled her out the door and down the stairs.

"Your buttons can wait. And when you get home at noon, we'll have to have a little talk about priorities."

"What are pwi...pwiowi—"

"I'll explain later." Bundling Janey into her coat and mittens, Laura called out, "Kay, are you all set?"

"Coming!" Kay's voice came from the direction of the studio. "I'm just pouring Dean a cup of coffee. I thought he could use a break, so I invited him in."

Squeezing her eyes shut, Laura mouthed the vilest word she knew.

"Is Mr. Kettle-wing here?" Janey asked delightedly. "Can I say hi to—"

"*No.*" Laura yanked Janey's woolen cap on with a little too much force. "There's not enough time."

Kay came down the hall, shrugging on her colorful, fringed blanket coat. "You ready, sweetie?" she asked Janey.

"Only just," Laura said. "Your little psychologist's trick of leaving her on her own has produced surreal-istically disastrous results."

Kay shrugged as she opened the front door, hus-tling Janey out ahead of her. "Now you know why I don't believe in psychology anymore."

Laura grabbed Kay's arm as she was leaving and rasped, "You invited him in for coffee?"

"I was sure you'd want to thank him for chopping all that wood for you," Kay responded with a guile-less smile as she closed the door behind her.

Laura stared at the door, thinking, *I really am gonna kill her. It's not just a joke anymore.*

Steeling herself, she turned and made her way back to the studio.

And Dean.

8

DEAN HEARD HER come up slowly behind him as he stood contemplating the roughed-out painting of Janey, while sipping coffee from a heavy, obviously handmade mug. He wondered if Laura had made it; he recalled her taking one or two pottery classes at Rutgers.

She cleared her throat. "Uh, thanks for chopping that wood, but I'd rather you didn't do any more. I'll finish it up myself. I don't mind."

"Sure you do," he said without turning around. "You told me so."

"I really didn't mean—"

"This is wonderful," he said, nodding toward the painting.

That seemed to catch her off guard, because it took her a moment to respond. "It's...unfinished. I just started it. It won't look like that when it's—"

"I know." Smiling, he glanced at her over his shoulder, to find her standing in the open doorway with her arms tightly crossed, her expression pensive. She looked ridiculously pretty in her paint-spattered apron, the same one she'd had in college. She'd caught her hair up haphazardly in one of those claw things, but rebellious tendrils had sprung free to curl around her face and tumble down her nape. Her face, with its exquisitely translucent skin, struck him as unusually pale at present, or maybe it was just an effect of the lighting—those merciless overhead fluorescents augmented by the sunlight streaming through the south-facing wall of windows.

Realizing he was staring at her, he returned his attention to the painting. "That pose is terrific. You've captured her little-kid awkwardness, and that makes it more...I don't know, more *real* than one of those idealized kids in their Sunday best with their hands folded in their lap. It's really *Janey*, you know? Not some generic kid from central casting." Turning to face her, he said, "You've still got it, Lorelei."

Color rose in her cheeks, which he found absurdly gratifying. "Thanks," she murmured, looking away.

"Since when have you been into painting people?" he asked, eyeing about a dozen canvases stacked against one wall, a handful of which were portraits, mostly of Janey. Laura used to just paint the ocean, with the occasional landscape or still life thrown in for variety.

"It, uh, it started when Janey was born," she said tentatively, without budging from her rigid stance in the doorway. "The first time I sketched her, it was in the hospital a couple of hours after I delivered her." She looked toward a picture hanging on the wall above her worktable.

He smiled when he got close enough to see that the drawing, although double-matted and beautifully framed under glass, had been executed in ballpoint pen on a creased white institutional paper napkin. With fluid, economical strokes of the pen, Laura had perfectly captured the image of the newborn Janey fast asleep, her thumb snugged firmly into her mouth, her hair sprouting out of her head in a way that made her look uncannily like Sid Vicious.

Dean said, "I'm surprised you had the wherewithal, so soon after giving birth, to draw this. I, uh...I take it the delivery went okay, and all that."

She rubbed her arms. "Yeah, basically. It was a pretty long labor, thirty-eight hours."

Dean winced reflexively. "Ah, Laura..." He took a step toward her.

She shrank back, just fractionally, but it was enough to stop him in his tracks.

He rubbed the back of his neck. "It must have been..." Been what? Hard? Lonely? Terrifying? "I'm sorry, honey, I'm..."

Her gaze flicked toward him and then away at the involuntary endearment.

"Did you have anyone..." Why was this so hard? he wondered. Because he felt ashamed. Because he should have been there for her and wasn't. "Your grandmother was already gone, right? Was anyone there with you?"

She nodded. "Kay. I'd only known her about a month and a half, but we'd become tight in a really short time. She was great, helped me with my breathing and all that. She was there for the whole thing. They even let her cut the cord." With a little chuckle, Laura added, "I think they thought we were, like, *life partners*, you know?"

He smiled, too, at the notion of his little Lorelei, the straightest of the straight arrows, being taken for a lesbian with a turkey baster pregnancy. He could see it with the eccentric Kay, but Laura?

"I still paint mostly seascapes," Laura said, "even in the winter. They're my livelihood, after all, and what I most love to paint. But I've really gotten into painting Janey. Not to sell, of course, just for myself."

"That's great. Sure beats an album full of snapshots."

"Oh, I've got plenty of those, too. Janey, she's..." Laura shrugged a little self-consciously. "She's sort of taken over my life—in a good way. Having her has changed everything."

A cumbersome silence descended between them. Dean took a sip of coffee, and then another, looking around curiously at this makeshift painting studio that had changed so little in six years, and which looked and felt and smelled so much like his Lorelei.

My Lorelei... Since when had she been his?

Who was he kidding? *Since always. Since forever.*

He noticed a shabby old club chair in the corner; that was new. "Mind if I sit?"

She looked toward the chair, hesitated.

"You can get back to the painting," he said, lowering himself into the big, squishy chair and resting an ankle on the opposite knee. "I don't want to interfere with your work. I wouldn't mind watching you for a few minutes, though, while I finish this." He took a sip of coffee, his gaze trained on her.

She studied the floor for a moment, her forehead creased, then unfolded her arms and turned toward her worktable. "Suit yourself."

Drawing in a deep, lingering breath, he said, "I love the way it smells in here."

Her expression softened slightly as she set about fiddling with tubes and jars. "Me, too."

He drank his coffee in silence, but slowly, to make this visit last. Laura dipped a brush in the pink she'd mixed up, turned toward the painting and applied the color in light, cautious strokes to Janey's cheeks.

When she finally spoke, it was to ask him how long he'd been living aboard the *Lorelei*.

"Four years," he answered. "Ever since I got out of the air force."

"You used to say they were going to end up court-martialing you for being such a nonconformist," she said. From where Dean sat, his view of her was in profile, so he could see that she was smiling, sort of. "I take it that never came to pass."

"Nah, turns out they didn't much mind me pushing the envelope as long as I didn't punch right out of it. In fact, I was just about to make captain when I opted out."

"So, why'd you opt out?" Standing back from the canvas, Laura inspected her work.

He shrugged, took another sip of coffee. "It was never a perfect fit for me—you know that. And then, after what happened to Will..."

She continued to stare at the painting, but Dean could tell from the distant look in her eyes that she wasn't seeing it.

"After that," Dean said, "I started counting the days. All I wanted was to get out and not have to deal with anybody or anything but me."

Her jaw set, Laura exchanged her flat brush for one

shaped like a fan. She went to work again, gradually blending the pink into the flesh tone with the dry brush until Janey's cheeks were so perfectly suffused with color that they looked as if they'd be hot to the touch.

"You've become quite the hermit," she observed as she painted. "Kay and I had a heck of a time finding you. No address, no phone, no e-mail account..."

"I keep a post office box in Portsmouth, but all I ever get is the occasional junk mail. And I don't like to own stuff that's just going to complicate my life, like phones and computers."

"You don't even have a car, do you? You said you'd rented one to drive down here. How do you get around on dry land?"

"Believe it or not, I've still got that old Sportster."

"You're kidding." She grinned in evident disbelief.

"Nothing's changed very much with me, I guess."

Her grin faded. Turning back to the table, she started fussing with things again, but in a preoccupied way, as if she were just trying to avoid him.

Setting his mug on the table, Dean rose from the chair and pulled the crinkled green envelope out of his back pocket.

She groaned when he held it out to her. "Dean, I thought you'd given up on trying to make me take that money. That's what you said yesterday."

"This is the last time, I promise. Just one last chance."

She held her hands up. "Dean..."

Capturing one of her wrists, he shoved the envelope into her hand. "Take it, Laura. Make this easy. I want you to have it. Not just for you, but for Janey."

She tried in vain to pull away from him. "*Please* don't bring Janey into this."

"Will would have wanted her to have—"

"Or Will." With a furious yank, she wrested her arm free. "Especially not Will."

Dean clenched his jaw.

"Here." She extended the envelope to Dean. "I don't want it."

He rested his hands on his hips. "Neither do I."

"Fine." She dropped it into a trash can filled with grimy rags. "That settles it. Now, if you don't mind, I have work to do."

Seizing her by the upper arms, he compelled her to meet his gaze. "Why won't you take the money, Laura?"

"Why are you so determined to give it to me?"

He closed his eyes and heard it again, the roaring explosion in the middle of the night, followed by the screams of his comrades. He felt the shock of finding Will, lying in his own blood, his chest torn open by a terrorist's bomb, and the grief that had consumed him as he'd cradled his friend in his arms, waiting for the inevitable. It hadn't taken long, a minute or two....

Opening his eyes, he said, "Will made me promise something before...he died."

She just stared at him.

Dean drew his hands gently down her arms, and up again. "He asked me to take care of you."

Her forehead creased. "Take care of..."

"You know, make sure you had a roof over your head, that you were provided for..."

She nodded, but he knew what she was thinking: that he hadn't exactly done a bang-up job of taking care of her. In fact, after walking out on her six years ago, he'd pretty much completely ignored her. That he'd done it because he knew she'd be better off without a screwup like him in her life did little to assuage his guilt for having abandoned her that way—especially after having taken advantage of her in her time of grief, thereby betraying both her and Will in a single act of supreme selfishness.

But to voice any of that would be to reopen old wounds that were best left alone. He couldn't undo what he'd done that night. But he could try to make up for it, even if it was too little too late.

"The money..." He stroked her arms lightly, grateful just to be able to touch her. "It's my way of saying I'm sorry for leaving you alone all those years after promising Will I'd look after you. I figured I owed it to you—to you and Janey—to try and make up for those years."

"You don't owe me anything," Laura said, looking him squarely in the eye for the first time that morning. She spoke quietly and deliberately, as if she were choosing her words with care. "I know you...you must find this hard to believe, but you've already given me more than you can imagine."

"Laura, that's nuts." Gentling his voice, he trailed the back of his hand down her cheek, which felt as soft as Janey's. "What have I ever given you but grief?"

She smiled enigmatically. "Trust me, Dean. I haven't been shortchanged in our relationship."

Relationship. Dean had never thought of what he had with Laura as being a "relationship."

"You've been more than shortchanged," he said bitterly. "You've been victimized—by me. I've treated you…" He released her to claw his hands through his hair, cautioning himself not to get into it, not to tear open those old, mostly healed wounds. "Laura, I know money can't buy happiness, but it can buy solutions to lots of the little problems that plague a person's life, like leaky roofs and deteriorating porches. God, Laura, it would make everything so much simpler if you would just take this check."

"Not for me." Reaching into the trash can, she retrieved the green envelope—now oil stained—and held it toward him. "It would only complicate things for me, only make me…regretful about things I shouldn't regret."

"Laura, please…"

"Take it. Please. It's yours. Use it to buy solutions to the problems that plague your own life."

Dean mulled that over for a moment, smiling to himself when it dawned on him that the biggest problem in his life right now was how to finally live up to his pledge to Will to look after Laura. He *could* use this money to fulfill that pledge, even if she wouldn't take it outright.

"All right." He accepted the envelope from her, folded it in half and stuck it back in his pocket. "You win. I'll put this in the bank today."

Those astute golden eyes of hers narrowed on him. "I win? Just like that?"

"Just like that," he said with a smile.

9

LAURA DRIFTED AWAKE to an incessant bang-bang-banging that she at first blearily assumed was coming from inside her own skull. She pulled the quilt over her head, which muffled the noise—a steady hammering from overhead that seemed to fill up her bedroom—but did nothing to dampen the scalding headache that still plagued her after...

Poking her head out from under the covers, she checked the alarm clock on the nightstand, which said it was 9:47 a.m. That meant over twelve hours had passed since she'd taken to her bed with a pounding head and crippling fatigue.

It had been a rough week—that's why she felt so lousy. Or at least that was what she'd told herself last night. Dean's unexpected arrival last Sunday had thrown the emotional equivalent of a Molotov cocktail into her orderly little world. She'd spent the past six days trying to avoid him—a mostly futile effort, given the way Kay kept contriving to bring them together.

And not just Kay, but Janey, albeit with no ulterior motive other than to spend as much time as possible in the company of "Mr. Kettle-wing." Dean had asked her to call him by his first name, but Laura had vetoed that familiarity, which of course had made her feel like the Bitch Queen of Port Livingston—just one more irritation atop a heap of others.

Bang bang bang. Bang bang bang. Bang bang...

With a growl of exasperation, Laura threw back the covers and sat up, igniting an electric bolt of pain in her head, underscored by a firestorm of stabs and twinges throughout her body. What had been mere fatigue last night was morphing into something altogether more ominous.

Don't think about it. Laura got out of bed and, shivering violently in her flannel nightgown, wrapped herself in her comfy old chenille robe. She shouldn't be cold; it had been increasingly pleasant all week, during which the remaining snow had melted, and today it was supposed to get into the low sixties. *You're fine. Just tired.*

Not to mention emotionally ravaged from Dean's sudden reappearance in her life.

Bang bang bang...

It *was* coming from overhead, she realized. Someone was banging on the roof of her house.

What now? She padded downstairs, keeping a firm grip on the banister because her legs felt about as sturdy as overcooked linguine. Shoving her feet into the duck boots she kept by the back door, she went outside, where she found Dean's dark green Jeep parked in the driveway, a stack of asphalt roofing shingles on the ground next to it. Her tall stepladder was propped against the house.

Yanking her robe more tightly around herself, she strode farther out into the yard, turned and squinted up at the roof, raising a hand to shield her eyes against the hazy morning sunlight. Her shivering worsened when she saw Dean crouching up there like an oddly graceful gargoyle, hammering a tile in place. He wore a baseball cap today over hair that had been pulled back into a ponytail.

"Dean, what are you—" Her words scraped her throat, inciting a fit of hacking coughs.

Dean clambered to the edge of the roof. "Laura? Oh, God, I woke you up. I'm sorry—I didn't think you were home. Your car's not here."

"I left it at the shop last night," she said hoarsely. "Kay drove me home."

"You should have had me look at it. You know I can fix just about anything."

"Not this. I need a whole new transmission."

"You need a whole new *car*. That old junker's gonna implode one of these days."

"Very astute, but all I can afford right now is the transmission." Barely. "Dean, what are you doing up there? Are you repairing my roof?"

"No."

She frowned at the hammer in his hand, wondering if her mystery malady was making her hallucinate.

"I'm replacing it," he said with a smile.

Laura closed her itchy eyes and rubbed them.

"It's all your fault for making me stop smoking," he explained. "I've got to do *something* to keep from going stir-crazy. Oh, and I'm going to be taking care of that porch of yours, too, but before I buy the supplies, I thought I'd see if you wanted me to maybe screen it in for you."

"I want you to maybe leave it the heck alone! *And* the roof!"

"If you're worried about me doing it right, don't. I did this kind of stuff in college, remember?"

"It's not that, it's...it's..." Laura let loose with a sneeze that jolted her.

"Hey, are you okay?" he asked. "You look like hell."

"No, I don't," she claimed indignantly, despite the racking shudders that gripped her.

"No, you do. What's the matter? You sick?"

"I might be coming down with a cold," she allowed. "Dean, why are you replacing my roof?"

"I like to keep busy. You don't look good. Are you sure it's just a cold?"

"How much did this stuff cost?" she demanded, gesturing toward the stack of shingles.

"It's a present from me to you."

"How much did it cost, Dean?"

"Didn't your mother ever tell you it's not polite to ask the cost of a present?"

A hoarse little bark of frustration escaped Laura. "Stop this! You shouldn't be doing this!"

"Tell you what," he said, raising a placating hand. "I'll stop for now so you can get some sleep, but as soon as you feel better—"

"As soon as I feel better," she croaked, "I'm going to get a restraining order issued that says you can't come within a hundred yards of me or my roof ever again! Or my porch!" Amid another tubercular coughing fit, she turned and stomped into the house.

"Laura!" Dean called after her. "Laura, you really don't look good. Are you sure it's just a—"

She slammed the back door behind her, kicked her boots across the kitchen and stalked upstairs, muttering invectives about Dean Kettering all the while. Checking out her reflection in the bathroom mirror, she had to concede that Dean had a point: she did look like hell, with her pallid complexion and fright-wig hair. Splashing water on her face and brushing her teeth so exhausted her that all she could think of as she left the bathroom and padded barefoot to her room was getting back into bed and becoming unconscious as quickly as possible.

"Hey, Lorelei."

She squealed when she encountered Dean in the hallway. "Wh-what are you doing here?"

"I'm worried about you. You don't look good."

"So you've said. Listen, I told you—I'm fine. It's just a little cold."

Removing his baseball cap, he closed his hands around her shoulders and touched his lips lightly to her forehead. They felt so cool and soft that she grew dizzy, thinking, *Don't stop. Let's stay here, just like this, until I'm better....*

"You've got a fever, a bad one, I think. Have you got a thermometer?" He took her by the hand and led her into her bedroom, leaving his cap on the little table by the door.

"Yeah, there's one in a glass on the bathroom sink, but I really don't think I'm that sick. I can't be. I've got stuff to do."

"Yeah, yeah, yeah," he said, reminding Laura of

Kay. "Here, let's get you into bed and see what kind of a temperature you're running. Then we can talk about all that stuff you've got to do."

Dean untied the sash to her robe, slid it off her and tossed it across the foot of the bed. She instantly started shaking again, whether from her fever or from the intimacy of his partially disrobing her, however innocently, she couldn't say. Pulling back the quilt and top sheet, he urged her to lie down, and raised the covers up to her chin.

"I'll be right back," he said, leaving the room. He had some folded papers sticking up out of his back jeans pocket, Laura noticed. She heard him in the bathroom; he returned moments later with her digital thermometer. "Open up," he coaxed, sitting on the edge of the bed and slipping the instrument into her mouth.

He stroked her hair, his gaze taking in the paintings of Janey on the walls, Grandma's beautiful old rolltop desk in the corner, the faded old flowered wallpaper and lace curtains, and finally the high, century-old four-poster bed. She wondered if he was thinking about the last time he'd been in this room, this bed.

His eyes met hers, and she knew that was exactly what he'd been thinking of.

Beep.

He slid the thermometer out of her mouth, frowning at the readout. "One hundred and two point seven. This isn't just some little cold, Laura."

She groaned when it came to her. "Marie—the clerk at the art supply store in Hale's Point—she told me she wasn't feeling so good, and that everybody in her family was sick in bed with the flu. That was two days ago."

"Thursday?"

She nodded.

"I was in Hale's Point Thursday, too," he said.

"What for?"

He hesitated, smiling in a way that almost looked nervous. "I'll tell you later."

"Dean..."

"That's it, then," he said, tucking the covers around her as if she were a child. "You've got the flu."

"You're changing the subject."

"My newest bad habit, remember? Maybe I should take you to the doctor."

She shook her head. "It's a virus—there's nothing she can do for me."

"I guess not," he conceded. "You need something to bring that fever down, though, and lots of fluids, and bed rest. No running around attending to all that stuff you claim you've got to—"

"Impossible." She shook her head, which only made it throb. "I've got to pick up Janey from Danielle's, then finish making her costume for this play she's in at church tomorrow. And after that—"

"Whoa, first things first. You've got to pick her up from where?"

"Her friend Danielle's—she spent the night and I've got to get her at eleven."

"I'll get her."

"No. No. Absolutely not."

Dean closed his eyes briefly. "Laura..."

"Please, Dean. I was handling things just fine before

you came along, with your million-dollar check and your roofing shingles and your sudden resolve to fix up my life. For your information," she said, her voice rustier with every word, "I don't need your help and I don't want your help. My life has been going along just swell without you."

Bracing his arms on either side of her, Dean leaned in closer, his transparent blue eyes searching hers. "Has it, Lorelei?"

She closed her eyes, which suddenly stung with heat. "Yes."

Her breath hitched in her throat when she felt his cool, work-roughened fingertips brushing her forehead, her cheek, her neck.

"'Cause my life..." he began. "I mean, it's all right, but sometimes I think maybe it's missing something. When I'm lying awake at night, I start thinking about it...I start thinking about *you*. And I wonder what would have happened if things had been different and—"

"Laura!" A voice from downstairs—Kay's voice— was accompanied by the slamming of the back door. "You here? I'm going into town. You need anything?"

Opening her eyes, Laura filled her lungs with air to call out a response, but Dean touched his fingers to her lips and said, "You shouldn't be straining your throat." Over his shoulder, he yelled, "She's up here, Kay. Would you mind bringing up a glass of water and some aspirin?"

There was a pause. "She hurt?"

"Sick." Turning back to Laura, he started trailing a hand through her hair, which made her eyes drift shut. "That's right," he murmured. "Just relax. You need to stay in this bed and be waited on hand and foot until you're better." His fingers grazing her scalp transported her into a realm of pure, soothing sensation; she felt as if she were floating. "So, uh...this Danielle, where does she live?"

Laura opened her eyes with an exasperated sigh. "No, Dean—I told you. I can't have you doing all this stuff for me."

"Are you saying you're going to go get Janey yourself? With a fever of almost 103 and—"

"It's only 102.7."

"—and no car?"

"Oh." *Right.* "Kay will do it," Laura said.

"What will I do?" Kay asked as she strode into the bedroom bearing a tray from Laura's kitchen, which held a pitcher of ice water, a glass, a bottle of aspirin, an orange and a thick slab of the banana nut bread Laura had made yesterday, slathered with butter. "Oh, Laura," she lamented when she came around to the other side of the bed and got a good look at her friend. "Honey, you look like hell."

"So I've been told." Laura grimaced as she painfully pushed herself into a sitting position, aided by Dean, who piled pillows behind her for her to lean against.

"She has the flu," Dean stated.

"I *thought* you looked a little peaked yesterday." Setting the tray on the night table, Kay pried open the cap on the aspirin bottle. "Down the hatch!" She shook two tablets into Laura's palm and filled the glass with ice water. "So, what are you volunteering me for?" she asked as Laura dutifully swallowed the pills.

"Someone needs to pick Janey up at Danielle's house at eleven," Laura said, handing the glass back.

"That's the house where we dropped her off yesterday, right?" Kay asked. "Sure—I'll do it."

"I told her I would," Dean said, "but she freaks out whenever I try to offer any help."

"She doesn't know what's good for her." Kay shot Laura a meaningful look. "Lucky for her—and Janey—that she's got sensible friends."

"Kay..." Laura moaned.

"Danielle lives in this big red house on the corner of Spencer and Main," Kay told Dean. "You can't miss it."

Laura sank back into the pillows, muttering, "I hate you both."

Smiling, Dean brushed stray locks of hair off her face. "Now, what's this about a play at church tomorrow?"

"I forget," Laura said petulantly.

"Janey's church school class is putting on a play about Moses for the congregation during the service tomorrow." Picking the orange up off the tray, Kay set about peeling it. "Janey plays the pharaoh's daughter—the one who finds the baby Moses in the basket."

"Her costume's not done yet," Laura said.

"It's just the headpiece that still needs work, right?" asked Kay, who had helped Laura design the elaborate Egyptian ensemble. "I can finish it up in ten minutes."

"Are you sure?" Laura asked.

Kay grinned. "Have hot glue gun, will travel."

Laura breathed a sigh of relief. "You're a lifesaver, Kay. Uh...just one other thing. I don't think I'm gonna be up to taking Janey to church tomorrow. I don't suppose you'd be willing to do it?"

"Oh." Kay frowned at the orange as she stripped off the last of its skin, undoubtedly dismayed at the prospect of having to sit through an entire church service. "Uh...isn't there someone in the congregation who can just, like, pick her up and drop her off?"

"Well, yeah, but Janey's been so excited about this play, and so eager for me to see it. I just thought if I couldn't be there for her, maybe you..." Laura swallowed down her disappointment; beggars couldn't be choosers, and Kay was usually so cheerful about helping out with Janey. "Forget it. It doesn't matter."

"Sure it does," Dean said. "You're right—one of us should be there for her."

One of us? Laura thought, both disturbed and touched that he was including himself among the significant adults in Janey's life. He'd known her for barely a week—although it was clear that the child adored him, an affection that appeared to be mutual.

Thinking about the instant rapport between Dean and Janey made Laura's head start thudding again. "No, that's all right, Dean. I'll ask Janey's church school teacher to take her."

He shook his head. "No way. I'm going to take her."

Laura rolled her eyes. "When's the last time you saw the inside of a church?"

Dean's expression softened, grew reflective. "Your wedding." He captured her gaze and held it. "It was this little Norman Rockwell-looking church here in Port Liv, on the town square." Softly he said, "You wore daisies in your hair, and this incredible gown that you'd made yourself. It was so simple, and I remember it had two or three layers of this really, really soft, thin material that looked even better when it got a little wrinkled...."

"Handkerchief linen," Laura murmured raspily.

He nodded, as if in a trance. "And you wore white ballet slippers, and a gold locket your grandmother gave you, and you carried daisies and black-eyed Susans mixed in with a whole big cloud of those little tiny frothy white flowers."

"Baby's breath."

He smiled into her eyes. "You were so beautiful. You blew me away."

Laura's heart trembled in her chest like a bird.

Kay broke the spell by clearing her throat. "Cool, so it's all set. Dean will take Janey tomorrow. It's First Presbyterian, Dean, the same church Laura got married in. The service is at ten."

"But...but Janey's got to get there half an hour early for makeup," Laura said. "Really, Dean, you don't have to do this."

"I want to." Dean gave her hand a squeeze. "I'll come by for her about a quarter after nine." Rising, he crossed to the door. "I'm going to go outside and clean up my mess before I head out to pick up Janey. Oh...hey, listen. Uh, this guy from Manson's Heating and Cooling might show up while gone. If he does, just ask him to wait till I get—"

"Whoa, time out!" Laura sat forward, her head not

so much throbbing as whirling and spinning. "Why would someone from Manson's Heating and Cooling be coming here?"

"It's nothing," Dean said, palms raised in a gesture of appeasement. "Just an estimate."

"For..."

With a sigh, Dean lifted his baseball cap from the table where he'd left it and snugged it back on. "A furnace and ductwork."

"*What?*"

"All *right!*" Kay exclaimed. "It's about time!"

"*No!*" Laura wailed. "Dean, you are *not* going to buy me a furnace! Do you hear me? I won't have it!"

"Since you're already in a frenzy of outrage..." He withdrew the folded papers from his back pocket. "You'd asked me what I was doing in Hale's Point the other day."

"Whatever it is," Laura said, "I don't want it. I don't want *any* of it."

"I'll take it!" Setting the peeled orange on the tray, Kay snatched the papers out of Dean's hand.

"Don't you see what he's doing?" Laura demanded of her friend.

"Sure," Kay said, unfolding the papers. "Since you won't take his million dollars, he's spending it on things you need." She scanned the document, cackling with glee. "Or just want a *whole* lot."

"What is it?" Laura asked.

"I'm outta here," Dean said quickly, backing out of the door. As he turned to sprint down the stairs, he called out, "Don't let her get too worked up, Kay. She should be resting!"

Laura turned to Kay. "Well?"

Grinning, Kay held the papers toward Laura. "It's the title to Raleigh Hale's boat, the one you've been wanting, the Precision 18."

"Oh, for crying out loud." Ignoring the papers, Laura slumped back into the pillows. "I can't accept it. I won't accept it."

Glancing at the title again, Kay said, "It's in your name. It's already yours."

"I can't *believe* you're aiding and abetting him!" Laura sputtered.

"And I can't believe you're trying to burn off this man who, in addition to being majorly hunky and an all around pretty cool guy, just happens to be the father of your child." Breaking a section off the peeled orange, Kay offered it to Laura, who waved it away.

"I wish you hadn't figured that out," Laura said. "I hope to God Janey never does."

"She shouldn't have to." Popping the orange section into her own mouth, Kay said around it, "You should just tell her."

"Yeah, right."

"Yeah. *Right.* She deserves to know who her father is. Just like Dean deserves to know he has a daughter. He feels a *bond* with her, Laura—it's obvious. Don't you feel guilty, not telling him?"

"God, of course I do! It's eating away at me. But we've been all through this. Dean just isn't father material, and he never will be."

"Jeez Louise, he's taking her to *church* tomorrow. How much more paternal can you get?"

"I'm not saying he can't play the role for kicks, but

sooner or later the novelty will wear off and he's going to vanish into thin air. That'll be hard enough on Janey when it happens. Think how much worse it'll be if she knows he's her actual, real, biological father. Plus, can you imagine trying to explain it to her? She assumes Will was her father. If I told her the truth now, she'd never understand why I kept it from her."

"Of course she would. No one appreciates better than a child how complicated life can get sometimes. They know about sticky situations and hard decisions. Just say, 'Janey, I've got something to tell you—something pretty huge.' If you explain it right, she'll understand." Kay handed her another wedge of orange.

This time Laura took it. "You're sounding an awful lot like a shrink again, Ms. I-don't-believe-in-psychology-anymore."

Kay shrugged as she broke off a slice for herself. "Old habits die hard."

10

"SO, HOW COME YOU decided to make a T-rex?" Dean asked Janey as he helped her reduce today's issue of *Newsday* into a mountain of six-inch-long strips. "Why not something a little—" he shrugged "—friendlier?"

"Fwendlier?" Janey cast him a skeptical look from the other side of the three-foot-high chicken wire infrastructure that she would transform today—with a little adult help—into a papier-mâché tyrannosaurus rex for a preschool project that involved making representations of their favorite animals. Spring having finally sprung on Long Island—today it was downright balmy, more like June than April—they had opted to work outside on the tarp-draped front porch, which Dean had almost completely rebuilt after finishing the roof.

It was three weeks ago that he had begun work on the roof, only to put that job on hold for several days while Laura got over her killer case of the flu—with some help from Dean, who had, as promised, waited on her hand and foot, in addition to taking care of Janey. To his surprise, he had actually enjoyed the Moses play, and the church service itself had been so unobjectionable that when Janey had asked him to attend Easter services with them last Sunday, he had readily agreed.

Meanwhile, Laura still fought him tooth and nail over every little favor he did, every purchase he made for her. The furnace and the boat were bad enough, but she'd really gone off the deep end when he'd parked that new maroon Chevy Blazer in her driveway and handed her the key. As far as he knew, she hadn't so much as stuck that key in the ignition, not once.

Nevertheless, she was clearly getting used to his being here—maybe even warming up to him a little. She used to freeze over when he entered a room. Now, more often than not, she actually smiled at him. And when Janey had asked if he could help with her T-rex, Laura had hesitated only briefly before acquiescing.

Modest progress, perhaps, but he welcomed it.

"I wouldn't call any of the dinosaurs exactly *fwendly*," Janey said.

"Oh, you know what I mean. What about that pet dinosaur on *The Flintstones?* Dino. What kind is he?"

Janey, wearing one of her mother's old paint-spattered T-shirts as a smock, regarded him with a mixture of pity and forbearance. "The cawtoon kind. He isn't *weal*," she explained patiently. "He's just a picture."

Dean bit his lip as he laid a new sheet of newspaper on the tarp and tore it top to bottom. "Yeah, I know that. I just meant he's a certain, you know...breed, or whatever."

"There was no bweed that lived at the same time people lived."

"I'm aware of that," Dean said, smiling to himself.

"Believe it or not, I probably know almost as much about dinosaurs as you do."

Janey looked relieved. "I was worried you might think there were dinosaurs that lived past the Mesozoic Ewa into the Cenozoic."

Dean chuckled self-consciously, humbled by the realization that he probably didn't even know *almost* as much about dinosaurs as this precocious five-year-old. "I might not remember the names of the eras and whatnot, but I do know they all died off. An asteroid, right?"

"That's one theowy," Janey said as she arranged her newspaper strips, for some reason, into a tidy stack.

"In the case of old T-rex here, I can't say as it was any great loss."

She looked up at him, her forehead furrowed. "What does that mean, 'any gweat loss'?"

"I mean, he was a pretty nasty guy, our friend here. You told me yourself he was the most feared meat-eater of all the dinosaurs."

"Well, of all the dinosaurs in the Cwetaceous Pewiod. But that's just 'cause he was good at feeding himself. That doesn't mean he was nasty."

"Admit it," Dean teased. "He was a bad, bad boy. He didn't play nice. Just filled his belly and thundered on to the next kill." Dean knew his own kind when he saw it.

"That doesn't mean he desewved to die off," Janey said with seemingly genuine passion. "He couldn't help being the way he was."

"Couldn't he?"

"No! Plus which, he might not have weally died off,

not the way you're thinking, anyway. He might have just changed."

Dean laughed. "You're saying a bad-ass like that—" He winced when he saw Janey squeal with laughter and cover her ears; he tried to keep his language clean around her, but sometimes he slipped. "Sorry. You're saying an antisocial fellow like Mr. Rex can turn over a new leaf and just decide one day that he doesn't want to rip other dinosaurs' heads off anymore?"

"It wasn't like that," she said with a giggle. "At the end of the Cwetaceous, some dinosaurs' bones started getting all hollow and stuff, and their hips kind of changed, and their mouths, and they started gwowing *feathers*—the fossils pwove it!—and *wings!*"

"Ah...you're saying this bad boy turned into a bird."

"It coulda happened. Mommy always says life is vast and mystewious." She cocked her head, smiling sagely. "Anything's possible."

Reaching around the chicken wire dinosaur, Dean ruffled Janey's hair. "You almost make me believe it."

The front door opened and Laura stepped onto the porch, wearing her ubiquitous paint-crusted denim apron over jeans and a T-shirt, and carrying a big steel bowl. "Who ordered the flour paste?"

Janey's arm shot up. "Me!"

"Here you are, *mademoiselle*." Laura set the bowl on the tarp near her daughter. *"Bon appétit."*

"It looks more like flour soup than flour paste," Janey said, sticking a finger in the creamy liquid.

"That's just what it's called. Here's how it works."

Squatting next to Dean, Laura chose a shred of newspaper from his pile and dipped it in the bowl. "You coat the strips with this goop, skim off the excess and lay them over the framework, like so."

"Ooh, can I twy?" Janey asked.

"It's your project," Laura said. "We're just your assistants."

Wiping her hands on a rag, Laura sat back on her heels to watch her daughter apply strip after strip to the chicken wire form, occasionally offering a little cursory help or a bit of advice, but for the most part just observing. Dean couldn't stop stealing glances at her when he didn't think she would notice. She seemed to glow in the soft sunlight permeating the porch, her skin radiant, her hair like burnished gold. But it was the unabashed pride glittering in her eyes that made her look exceptionally beautiful today.

Some women were born to be mothers—to nurture, to protect, to guide. Laura Sweeney was one of those women.

"My awms are getting tired," Janey complained when the framework was about half covered with papier-mâché. Rubbing her stomach, she added, "And I'm hungwy."

"Want me to take over for a while?" Laura asked, handing Janey the hand-wiping rag. "I can finish just the first layer, and then you can decide what to do from there."

"Gweat!" Janey bolted to her feet. "Are there any Oweos left?"

"They're in the Humpty Dumpty cookie jar," Laura said, adding, "Wash your hands first!" as Janey bombed through the front door and raced down the hall toward the kitchen.

Pulling the bowl closer to her, Laura started coating strips with the flour mixture and smoothing them onto the chicken wire. From the direction of the Sound came the caw-caw-caw of seagulls. A breeze wafted through the porch, fluttering the little strands of hair that had sprung loose from her single braid. She reached up and tucked them behind her ears, gingerly because her hand was covered with flour paste, but she left behind a little streak of it anyway, right on the crest of her cheekbone. Dean was tempted to wipe it away, if for no other reason than that it would give him an excuse to touch her, but it looked so oddly pretty that he decided to let it stay.

Just gazing at her made him feel slightly disoriented, but in a good way, as if his very soul were being rocked by the ocean.

"Here," Dean said, positioning the bowl between them. "Let me help."

"You've been awfully quiet," she said without looking at him. "Bored?"

"No." He smiled as he dipped a strip in the bowl and skimmed off the excess flour paste, which felt cool to the touch and slick between his fingers. "Just content, I think."

She did look at him then, a quick, curious glance, before returning her attention to the project. Of course she would think it odd to hear a rolling stone like Dean describe himself as "content." And yet he was.

And had been pretty much since his arrival in Port Livingston.

They worked in silence for a while—not an awkward silence, but not quite "companionable" either, charged as it was with the burdens of the past, the ambiguities of the present....

Laura didn't seem to notice her body brushing up against his as she leaned over to smooth down the coated newspaper strips; or maybe she did, and it didn't bother her. Dean hoped that was the case.

"So, when are you gonna break down and take that nice new Blazer of yours out for a drive?" he asked.

"After you leave," she said. "I'm going to return it to the dealer, but not till you've gone home to Portsmouth, 'cause otherwise I figure you'll just bring it back again. Same with Raleigh Hale's boat."

"What—are you gonna rip out the new furnace, too, and bash holes in the roof and the porch?"

She smiled a little grudgingly. "I'm not quite *that* up in arms about your little Daddy Warbucks campaign—almost, but not quite."

"That's *some* comfort." He shook his head as he molded papier-mâché strips onto the dinosaur's tail. "I'll just have to figure out how to spend the rest of the million on you in ways you can't undo. There's a lot of money left in the account. I'm gonna be a busy guy for the next month."

Laura reached for another newspaper strip; she wasn't smiling anymore. "You're really staying for a whole 'nother month?"

He nodded. "By then, it'll be toward the end of May, and time for me to get ready for my Bermuda trip. So you're stuck with me until then—unless you just let me give you the rest of the money, and then I'll be out of your hair."

She looked pensive as she applied that strip and another to the T-rex's belly. Was she actually considering putting an end to this farce by taking the money? Was she that eager for Dean to be out of her life?

Don't take it, Dean found himself silently beseeching—ironic, considering how anxious he had been for her to accept the money when he'd first offered it to her. But things had changed in the past month. He'd gotten used to being here; he didn't want to leave, not yet. His psyche, attuned for so long to the solitary rhythms of the sea, had become accustomed to a different, more communal rhythm. He liked being with Laura—and with Janey, too. He felt good in their presence—whole, complete...

Content.

Don't let it end yet. Not yet.

She turned to him, a smile flirting with the corners of her mouth. "If I took the money, just like that, it would be making things too easy for you. Given that you're going to force it on me whether I like it or not, I figure you might as well be as inconvenienced as possible."

He laughed, relieved. "You've become quite a vindictive little thing."

"Who said you're the only one who could grow and change?" She laid another couple of strips over the T-rex's belly. "So, you set sail around the end of May, then?"

"Yeah," he said, working his way toward the tip of the tail. "Setting out from New England, you really don't want to leave any earlier than that—and believe me, it's still pretty cold and wet till you hit the Gulf Stream."

"Let's see...Bermuda's in the middle of the Atlantic about—what?—six, seven hundred miles from New England?"

"A little more."

"So it takes how long to get there?"

"Singlehanding it like I do, it's about a week from Portsmouth to Saint George's Harbour. Less if there's not much wind and I end up falling back on the engine a lot, more if I have weather to deal with."

"I can't imagine enduring a trip like that all alone," she said.

He grinned. "I can't imagine enduring it with other people bumping into me every time I turned around. I prefer my autopilot for company." Although lately he'd been imagining what it would be like to take Laura along; it might not be so bad bumping into her every once in a while....

"You seriously don't get lonely, out there in the middle of the ocean with no one for company?" she asked, glancing at him as she smoothed down the patch of papier-mâché she'd just applied.

"Oh, there's company," he said. "Just not human company. You run across pods of dolphins from time to time, and they're pretty sociable guys. The Portuguese man-of-wars are a little more standoffish."

"Yeah, I can imagine," she chuckled.

"Then there's the occasional sea turtle that waddles on past—they're cool. Last year, on the inbound trip, I had a whale come up pretty close to the boat."

"Really? A whale? I would have loved to have seen that!" Laura went to dip a newspaper strip in the bowl of flour at the same time Dean did. She started when their hands touched.

He caught her wrist before she could draw away. "I would have loved for you to have been there."

Her cheeks pinkened as he took her hand, coated with flour paste, between both of his.

"I...thought you didn't like having other people aboard," she said.

"You're not 'other people.' You're...you've always been..." He rubbed her hand between his, savoring the warmth and softness of her skin through the slippery flour paste. "You appreciate things that not everyone appreciates. That's why your paintings are so...powerful, so arresting. You see beyond the surface. You see *into* things, right down to their essence...like that glassy green in the core of a wave as it rears up right before it crashes, or the feverish pink that kind of blooms up into Janey's cheeks while she's sleeping."

Laura tried to pull her hand away, but Dean held on tight.

"After you cross the Gulf Stream," he told her, "the water turns so blue, it's almost like you're looking into a swimming pool at night—you know, when it's lit up from underneath? You'd love that. You could bring your paints, and some canvases, and—"

"Dean..."

"And you wouldn't believe how bright the stars are at night, with no lights around for hundreds of miles. I've lain on the deck of the *Lorelei* and watched the

Milky Way sprawling all the way across the sky, like a hundred thousand diamonds. There's not another soul on earth I'd want lying there next to me except for you. Maybe I shouldn't be telling you these things, but—"

"No." She did pull her hand away then. "You shouldn't."

"Laura..." He closed a hand over her shoulder as she started to rise, getting flour paste on her T-shirt; she didn't seem to notice. "If I were to ask you to come with me..."

"I'd say no." She lifted his hand from her shoulder, but surprised him by holding on to it. "I'd have to say no."

"Because of Janey? Maybe we could take her along."

"You're kidding, right? On a trip like that?"

She had a point. "The two of you could fly out and meet me in Bermuda, then. I usually stay about two weeks. It's so beautiful there. You'd love—"

"I hate flying, remember? Plus, Janey will still be in preschool."

"Yeah, but..." He shrugged. "It's only *preschool*. But if you really didn't want her to miss the time, Kay could look after her while you're gone. I'm sure she'd be happy to."

"Yeah, but I've never been away from Janey for that long. And I still don't fly."

"At all?"

"Ever. I hate it."

"Maybe you should try to overcome that fear."

"Look, it's not about flying, Dean, and it's not about Janey. It's..." She looked away, shaking her head.

"This is about...that night, isn't it?" he asked, broaching the subject openly. "About what we...what I did that night six years ago, when I came here to—"

"What *we* did," she said tightly, staring into her lap. "I was just as responsible as you were."

"Well..." He cradled her hand in his. "I would argue that point, but the bottom line is you feel like you betrayed Will that night. And since I was the instrument of that betrayal, you don't want to have anything to do with me—or my money, even though it could make a big difference in your life. And Janey's."

Sliding her hand out from between his, she said, "Please don't keep bringing Janey up. This situation...it's not as simple as you think. It's not about betrayal, not really. I mean, it's true, I felt guilty about...what happened that night, but I also felt..." She met his gaze with a kind of serene resignation. "I felt as if it had to happen, that it was destined to happen. Like nothing could have stopped it."

What was it she'd told him in Portsmouth? *I wouldn't undo it even if I could.*

"Yes." Gripping her shoulders, he drew her closer. "There's always been this...this *thing* between us, this connection. I tried to walk away from it—from you. But the inevitable can't be denied. Fate can't be resisted."

"Yes, it can," she whispered unsteadily. "Sometimes it should."

"Why do you keep pushing me away?" he demanded a little too stridently, clutching her with a little too much force. "Why won't you take the damned money? Why won't you let me near you? It's been six years, Laura. Will is gone. I'm here."

"For how long?"

That caught him up short; he hesitated, grappling with a response.

"Connection or no connection, you and I were never meant to be," she said, her resignation flavored this time with sadness. "Not because of Will. I told you, it's not about Will. Like I said, it's complicated."

Dean pulled her closer, drilled his gaze into hers. "Explain it to me."

"I can't." She tried vainly to squirm out of his clutches. "I know you don't understand...."

"That's what you said to me in Portsmouth." This was exasperating, maddening. "If it's true, why the hell don't you just *explain* it to me?"

"I told you—I can't." She shook her head, her eyes shining wetly. "I can't!"

"Why not? What are you keeping from me, Laura?"

"Please, Dean..." She wrested her head to the side.

He took her by the chin and turned her to face him. Her cheeks were damp with tears. "Oh, honey..."

"Please...I can't." Her shoulders shook as he gathered her up and held her tight. "I can't explain it."

"Shh, it's all right," he soothed, cradling her head against his chest. "It's all right. I pushed too hard."

"Don't ask me to explain it," she begged, clutching his T-shirt as she soaked it with her tears.

"I won't," he murmured, kissing the top of her head. "I'll let it go. I promise. I'll let it go."

He held her, rocking her and stroking her hair, until

her weeping subsided. When she was calm again, she said, "I'm sorry, Dean. I'm really, really sorry."

"Shh..." He kissed the top of her head, tightened his arms around her. "You have nothing to be sorry about."

After a long pause, she whispered something that sounded like, "I wish that were true."

11

"HELLO!" Laura called out as she opened Kay's front door and strode into the foyer. Checking her watch, which revealed that it was 9:20 p.m., she winced. She'd lost track of time, having gotten way too wrapped up in her painting, as usual. Poor Kay had been baby-sitting Janey since early this afternoon, on top of having to pack for the vacation she took with her mother every year at the end of May—a bit of postwinter rejuvenation before Memorial Day weekend, when the tourists swarmed into Port Liv, filling the Blue Mist to capacity throughout the summer.

"You're late." Kay's breathless voice came from the top of the stairs. "And for the last Chick Flick Night of the season. Shame on you." She came into view, hauling a gigantic and obviously heavy tapestry-printed duffel bag down the stairs.

"Need any help with that?" Laura shucked off her cardigan and hung it on the coat tree, then kicked off her sneakers, leaving herself barefoot.

"Nah, we'd just end up tripping over each other." Having wrestled the duffel downstairs, Kay shoved it with a foot into a corner of the foyer.

"Is Janey in bed yet?"

"I got her into her jammies, but I haven't had the

chance to tuck her in yet. She's in the kitchen with Dean. She asked if he'd play barbershop with her."

"Barbershop?" That was a new one on Laura.

"Listen," Kay said, "about Janey. We can put her to bed upstairs, as usual, but I just checked my tickets and realized I'm gonna have to set out for La Guardia at, like, five o'clock tomorrow morning."

"Yikes! You want to cancel Chick Flick Night?"

"No way! I haven't seen *Casablanca* in years, and Dean, of course, has *never* seen it."

Which came as no surprise to Laura. One thing they'd learned from having shared Chick Flick Night with Dean for the past seven weeks was that he'd seen incredibly few movies in his lifetime.

"Anyway," Kay said, "you're best off bringing Janey home tonight after the movie."

"No problem. So." Laura nodded toward the over-stuffed duffel. "You all ready for your trip?"

Spreading her arms, Kay gazed heavenward with a transcendent expression. "Ten days in the Greek Islands. I couldn't possibly be any readier."

"I envy you." Laura would give anything to trade places with Kay, whose well-heeled mother liked to treat her to exotic vacations a couple of times a year.

"I did invite you and Janey to come with us," Kay reminded her.

"We've been all through this," Laura said, raising her hands to stave off a reprise of their recent debates on the subject. "I can't afford it and no, I am *not* going to break down and take that money from Dean, no matter how much of a pest you become. Plus, going to Greece means flying, and I don't do that."

"Phobias should be confronted, Laura."

"More brilliant psychological revelations from the supposed ex-shrink."

"Fine." Kay shrugged with overstated indifference. "It's best that you're here, anyway, in case Dean has any trouble playing reservations clerk." She usually drafted Laura to check her messages and return the calls of prospective guests when she went away. This year, Dean had agreed to do it, in exchange for free room and board for the remainder of his stay. "Remember, I'll be coming back Sunday, May 27, if anyone needs to speak to me personally."

"I'll remember." Heading for the kitchen, Laura said, "We'd better get this show on the road or you'll sleep through your alarm tomorrow morning. I'll put Janey to bed, you make the popcorn."

"I always make the popcorn," Kay groused as she unzipped her duffel and poked around inside it. "How about you do that while I tuck Janey in?"

"Deal," Laura said as she opened the kitchen door. "I'll send her out to..." She stood motionless in the doorway, staring openmouthed. "Uh..."

Dean was lazing back in a kitchen chair in the middle of the floor, his blue-jeaned legs stretched out and crossed at the ankles, his arms folded beneath the towel draped over his shoulders, his eyes half-closed. On a step stool behind him stood Janey, clad in her favorite dinosaur pajamas, her hair in two braids, frowning in concentration as she snipped away at Dean's hair with a pair of children's safety scissors. Hanks of that hair were scattered around her on the tiled floor. What little remained on Dean's head varied dramatically in length and stuck out at all angles, making him look like a particularly depraved punk rocker.

"Uh, Janey..." Laura began as she slowly entered the kitchen. "What are you doing, monkey?"

"Playing barbershop!" Janey announced, holding up her scissors in one hand and a freshly severed lock of hair in the other.

Dean gave Laura a sleepy-eyed smile. "Man, I forgot how good it feels to get your hair cut."

"Uh...Dean?" Circling around to face him, Laura stared unblinkingly at his...head. "You do know she's been using real scissors."

"Well, *duh.* How else could she cut my hair?"

Laura rubbed her forehead. "Have you looked in a mirror since she went to work on you?"

"Jeez, you are so uptight sometimes." Reaching out languidly, Dean grabbed Laura's hand and gave it a playful little shake. He'd been doing that more and more over the past couple of weeks—touching her casually for no reason in particular, as if she were some skittish young animal he was trying to tame. "Lighten up, Lorelei."

"Yeah, lighten up, Mommy!" Janey echoed, then dissolved in giggles at having chastised her own mother.

Shaking her head as if to clear it, Laura looked around for something reflective. She spied the shiny new stainless steel percolator Kay had bought herself when she'd decided she didn't like dripped coffee anymore, brought it over to Dean and held it in front of his face. "Check it out, wise guy."

"Oh, hey, cool!" he said, taking the percolator from her and holding it this way and that while he inspected himself in its gleaming surface. "It's like a fun-house mirror!"

"Let me see!" Taking the appliance from Dean, Janey peered, wide-eyed, at her own distorted reflection. "Cool! What's a fun house?"

Reaching behind him, Dean tugged on one of Janey's braids. "A place where you have fun, silly."

"Like Aunt Kay's house?" Janey asked. "Since you've been here, it's been *way* fun," she exclaimed, spreading her arms wide.

"It has for me, too, monkey," Dean said over his shoulder. "And by the way, you did an *awesome* job on my hair—you're a natural." He smiled at her. It was a fond, reassuring smile.

Downright paternal.

Laura felt suddenly off balance, as if the real world were just as contorted and surreal as the reflection in that damned coffeepot. "Give me that," she said, lifting it out of Janey's hands and setting it back on the counter. "Janey, you're up almost half an hour past your bedtime. Aunt Kay's going to tuck you—"

"But I'm not finished with Mr. Kettle-wing's hair!" she wailed. "I have to even it up."

"I'll even it up," Laura said, taking the safety scissors out of Janey's hand and slipping them in the front pocket of her jeans.

"But..."

"She'll just be doing the finishing touches," Dean told Janey, chucking her under the chin. "You did the important part."

With a sigh, Laura said, "That's right, monkey." She hefted her daughter off the step stool, gave her a big squeeze and set her down. "And Mr. Kettering's right—you did an excellent job."

"Weally?"

"Really. I'm sorry I didn't tell you that sooner."

Janey rewarded her belated stab at graciousness with a hug and a kiss on the cheek. "G'night, Mommy." Laura found herself unsettled when Janey turned to Dean and gave *him* a good-night kiss and hug, too.

After Janey left, Dean said, with a smile, "She almost makes me wish I had kids of my own."

Laura filled her lungs with air and let it out slowly. Forcing her mouth into the shape of a smile, she nodded toward Dean's grotesque new hairdo. "What do you say I clean that up for you?"

"Just a little off the top," he said, settling back in the chair again. "I wouldn't want you compromising Janey's artistic vision."

Sorting through Kay's utility drawer, Laura came up with a nice, sharp pair of grown-up scissors. "I can't believe you let her do that to you," she said as she shoved the step stool aside and positioned herself behind Dean.

He lifted his big shoulders in an indolent shrug. "It's just hair. It'll grow back."

"Very philosophical." Laura finger-combed Dean's hair this way and that, trying to figure out how to repair the mess.

"Mmm, that feels great," Dean murmured, his eyes drifting shut. "Do that some more."

"I never realized what a hedonist you are," Laura said as she set about trimming off the really bad parts.

Dean smiled without opening his eyes. "Then you haven't been paying very close attention."

"Do you have a comb?" she asked as she separated sections with her fingers and took tentative snips.

"Upstairs in my room."

"Maybe you should get it. I really need a comb to do this right."

"Then do it wrong. I'm enjoying this too much to get up."

Laura shook her head ruefully. He really did live for the moment. "There's a barber in town. You can get him to fix this up tomorrow."

"Too much like work."

"Aren't you at all worried about what your hair's gonna end up looking like?"

A groggy little huff of laughter escaped him. "It's not like there's some dress code for my lifestyle. I'm not gonna kick myself off the *Lorelei* for having a bad haircut."

His mentioning the *Lorelei* reminded her that they were in the third week of May already, and he'd always planned to be gone by the end of the month. "You, uh...you'll be heading to Portsmouth when Kay gets back from her vacation, I guess. Then off to Bermuda?"

Opening his eyes, he looked at her, his electric blue gaze making her breath catch in her throat. "That's the plan."

Laura nodded distractedly as she worked. "You realize you haven't spent the whole million on me yet.

Not that I've been keeping a strict tally, but I can guestimate with the best of 'em, and I don't think you're even close. Plus, you should know that, as soon as you leave, I'm going to be returning all that stuff you bought me—the Blazer, the boat, the riding lawnmower, the snowblower, those tools, the dishwasher, the microwave, the new furniture, all of it."

He expelled a long, lingering sigh. "Laura, honey, why are you such a pain in the ass?"

"Look, Dean...I told you right from the very beginning that I couldn't accept your money, but you've insisted on finding ways to make me take it. Obviously I can't do anything about the improvements you made to the house, but I can and will take back all that other stuff, and send you the money."

"Seems like an awful lot of trouble over nothing, but suit yourself." He closed his eyes again. "If you do that and send me the money, I'll just add it to Janey's trust fund."

Laura stopped cutting. "Trust fund?"

With his eyes still closed, he grinned. "Didn't I tell you about that? It's how I decided to solve the problem of not having spent the whole million on you before I leave. I'm setting up a trust fund for Janey that'll mature when she's eighteen. I went to Hale's Point and saw a lawyer about it yesterday. Once it's set up, he says there's no way you can undo it."

Laura let out an outraged little growl. "You just don't know when to stop, do you?"

"Never have." Gesturing toward his hair, he said, "Keep going. I'm enjoying this."

She stalked over to the counter, yanked the utility

drawer open and slammed the scissors back into it. "I'm done."

"How does it look?"

"Like shit." She slumped forward, her arms braced on the counter.

There came a pause. When Dean spoke, she realized he was right behind her. "Laura..." She felt his hands on her arms, stroking them lightly, up and down, through her white cotton shirt. "It's for *Janey*. Think about it. Think about the difference this money could make in her—"

"You don't understand," Laura moaned, shaking her head. How could she let him bestow all that money on Janey, given the magnitude of the secret she was keeping from him? And revealing that secret, regardless of Kay's advice, would only end in misery, especially for Janey, when Dean decided he'd had enough of experimenting with domestic bliss and it was time to move on—which was bound to happen sooner or later.

"No, you're right," Dean said quietly. "I don't understand. I'm not going to ask you to explain it to me again, because that only sets you off, but I *am* going to ask you to think about Janey and what's best for her. This lawyer I'm using to set up the fund has asked me to get her Social Security number and a copy of her birth certificate. That's all I need from you, Laura, and then Janey will be set for college and then some."

"Oh, God." Laura straightened up. Her birth certificate? That was all she needed, Dean seeing the telltale blank space next to "Name of father" on Janey's birth certificate. "I can't do that, Dean."

"Why not?" He said it softly, cajolingly, as he turned her around to face him. "Think about what's best for Janey."

"I am."

"Are you sure?"

"Why are you doing this, Dean? The new roof, the new car, the trust fund, all that *stuff*. Why?"

"I already told you," he said gravely. "I promised Will I'd take care of you, and it was about time I lived up to that promise."

Laura swallowed hard. "I know why you didn't. I know why you left that night, after we..." She dropped her gaze to the floor between them. "You were afraid I'd get all clingy, just because we'd...we'd..."

"What?"

"You thought I'd try and tie you down, and I don't guess I can blame you, knowing how I was—how I am—but you didn't have to just *sneak out* like that in the middle of the night. Do you have any idea how it hurt, after what had happened, to wake up and find you—"

"Yes. Yes. I do." Pulling her toward him, Dean enfolded her in his arms; she smelled the warmth of his skin, and the freshly laundered scent of his chambray shirt. "Oh, honey, yes. I've imagined what it must have been like for you a hundred times, and felt like a world-class heel every single time. It was inexcusable. But I didn't do it 'cause I didn't want to be with you. God, I'd *always* wanted to be with you."

"Then why..."

"Oh, Laura." Holding her tight, Dean kissed her on

the top of her head. "I went prowling around that night, after...after we made love, and I found..." His chest rose and fell. "I found your letter to Will, the one where you told him you were pregnant."

Laura closed her eyes. "Oh..."

"If I'd felt conflicted before, well..." He shook his head. "I was beside myself. I'd had no idea you were going to have a baby. That made it all so much worse, what I'd done to you—and him. You'd been consumed by grief—you didn't know what you were doing. But I did, and I went ahead and—"

"We were both responsible for that night," she insisted, meeting his gaze. "I told you that before. It was inevitable, meant to be."

Still holding her, he cupped her face, stroked a callused thumb over her cheek. "You had his child inside you. It didn't feel like it was meant to be. It felt wrong."

"Dean..."

"You were devastated afterward. You cried."

"I cried harder the next morning, when I woke up and found you gone. I did feel guilty, Dean, but that didn't mean..." She shook her head, frustrated with the inadequacy of words. "That didn't mean it was *wrong*, exactly. Just...complicated."

He nodded. "I guess I understand that now. I didn't then. I hated myself when I found that letter about the baby. I felt like a monster."

"You've always been too hard on yourself."

He sighed raggedly. "I decided you'd be better off without me in your life."

Laura's instinctive response was to tell him he was

wrong about that, but she held her tongue. Hadn't she herself concluded the same thing? "So, that's why I never heard from you again? Because you were protecting me from..."

"From me." He gathered her more snugly in his arms. "Yes. But then that million dollars came along, and now..."

And now...?

Laura looked up and found his face very close to hers, his gaze heartbreakingly earnest. "Not a day has gone by these past six years," he said, "that I haven't thought about you, wondering how your life was going, thinking about what might have happened if...things had gone differently for us."

Laura closed her eyes against the drunken riot of feelings coursing through her.

"Did you...think about me?" he asked.

"Yes," she breathed.

He buried his hand in her hair, gripped the back of her head, bringing her closer. "When Kay comes back and I...after I'm gone...will you miss me?"

Laura's delirium evaporated. He was leaving. Of course he was leaving. He would always leave. It was who he was; that would never change.

Still... "Yes," she whispered as he lowered his head to hers. "Yes. I'll miss you."

The kitchen door banged open. "You guys..."

Laura wrenched herself free from Dean's embrace, turned her back to him.

"I don't smell popcorn," Kay said. "What have you two been..." She gasped, then snorted with laughter. "Oh, my God! Dean! Whoa! Your hair!"

Laura turned to see Dean grinning sheepishly as he ran a hand through his inexpertly shorn hair. "What do you think?"

Crossing her arms, Kay appraised him with a critical expression. "I actually kinda like it. It's...different, all right, but... I don't know. Somehow, it suits you."

Strangely enough, on taking a good hard look at Dean, Laura had to admit that Kay had a point. He looked eccentrically handsome with that awkwardly cropped hair, which seemed to accentuate his keen-edged features and menthol blue eyes.

"Looks like Chick Flick Night's not gonna happen unless I crack the whip." Kay slid a bottle from her wine rack, grabbed a corkscrew out of the utility drawer and plucked three glasses off the overhead rack. "I'll go pop *Casablanca* into the VCR and uncork this lovely cabernet. Laura, you're still in charge of the popcorn, and Dean, if you wouldn't mind doing broom duty, inasmuch as that's your hair all over my kitchen floor..."

"At your service," Dean replied with a bow.

"I'm pushing the Play button in ten minutes," Kay announced as she crossed to the door. "Anyone who's not there when the movie starts will be sent to their room." Turning in the doorway, she added, with a devilish little smile, "Alone."

IT WAS DURING THE SCENE where a desperate Ilsa comes to Rick late at night, while her husband is at the political meeting, that Laura felt Dean's hand come to rest lightly on her bare foot.

She and Kay were sitting at opposite ends of the

burgundy velvet sofa in Kay's parlor, fleece throws draped over their laps, the half-empty popcorn bowl situated conveniently at the juncture of the two seat cushions. Dean had taken up his usual position on the floor between them, leaning back against the sofa with his legs stretched out on the Oriental rug.

Laura hadn't noticed him edging slightly closer to her—or rather, to her legs—until she felt his hand, warm and rough, molding itself to the top of her foot.

She started momentarily, anxious that Kay might see. Before the movie had started, while they were alone in the kitchen popping corn and sweeping up hair, Laura had made Dean promise not to do anything in front of Kay that might give her *ideas*. This situation was difficult enough without giving Kay—or, God forbid, Janey—the impression that there might be an actual *relationship* in the offing. Dean had agreed to keep his distance, yet now here he was touching her bare skin, and in a way that, even if not overtly sexual, felt all too familiar, all too intimate.

He must have sensed her tension, because he gave her foot a gentle, reassuring squeeze before smoothing his hand up her foot and then down again, as if trying to warm it. Looking down, Laura saw that his right hand, with which he was touching her, was entirely hidden by the fleece throw, along with most of his arm. Kay couldn't see what he was doing; she wouldn't be aware of it unless Laura said something.

So she didn't. Instead she lifted her wineglass from the end table and settled back to enjoy the rest of the movie.

Dean continued this nominally chaste caress

through the rest of *Casablanca*, his touch growing gradually more...sensually intrepid. He brushed his fingertips over her instep, slid his thumb beneath her foot to rhythmically massage her sole. Her heart skittered when he glided his hand up over her ankle and under the leg of her baggy jeans to gently knead her lower calf. By the time the movie ended, Laura felt a warm, liquid contentment that had a buzz of awareness to it, as if every cell in her body were humming.

She could barely look at Dean while they tidied up Kay's parlor and kitchen. She wouldn't meet his eyes when he held her sweater open for her, pointedly turned away from him to sit on the floor of the foyer while she put her sneakers back on. How utterly in his thrall she was, to have dissolved in sensual bliss just from having her foot fondled. She hadn't felt this level of aching desire since...

Since six years ago, when he had turned around on those stairs and stalked into her room with that look in his eyes....

"Earth to Laura," Kay said.

"What? Oh." Laura shook off her daze to find herself still sitting on the floor, staring at nothing. "Sorry, I'm...I guess I must be more tired than I thought." Dean offered her a hand; she took it and let him hoist her to her feet.

"I was telling you it's started to rain," Kay said. "And hard. Hear it?"

Laura groaned; it sounded like a real downpour. "I hate having to walk Janey home in this. Can I borrow an umbrella?"

"Sure," Kay said, "but what a shame to have to wake her up only to take her out in that."

"Then let's not wake her up," Dean said, grabbing his sweatshirt off the coat tree and zipping it on. "I'll carry her home. Laura, you can hold the umbrella over her. I bet she'll sleep right through it."

It sounded like a plan to Laura, so that's what they did. Janey, cradled in a quilt in Dean's arms and shielded by the umbrella, was dry and only partially roused from her slumber when Laura unlocked her front door and ushered them into the unlit house. She and Dean kicked off their wet sneakers, and then she followed him upstairs to Janey's room, pulling back the bedcovers so he could lay the child down. Janey stirred and opened her eyes as Laura was pulling the covers back over her. "Mommy?"

"Go back to sleep, monkey," Laura whispered, stroking her hair.

Janey nodded and closed her eyes.

Laura and Dean tiptoed out of Janey's room, closing the door behind them. They went back downstairs and stood for a moment in the darkened front hall, looking at each other.

"Thanks for doing that," she said, shivering in her damp clothes.

"No problem." He stuck his hands in his pockets. "Well, then, I guess I'll—"

"Um, would you like some coffee?" Laura asked. "Or a drink?"

"Coffee's good," he said. "Thanks."

She nodded. From the direction of the basement,

she heard her new furnace cycle on. "Okay, let's, uh..." She gestured toward the kitchen.

"Uh-huh." Dean started to follow her down the hallway.

"Oh, wait a minute." After only one step, she turned around, colliding with him. He grabbed her arms to steady her. It was so dark here that she could just barely make him out. "My sweater's soaked all the way through—it's dripping on the floor. Let me just..." She started tugging on the top button.

"Oh, sure."

Her hands were shaking so badly that she could barely manage to get the big wooden buttons through the buttonholes.

"Here..." He went to work on the buttons himself, pushing one after the other through its hole. His hands, as they brushed against her through the water-logged garment, seemed almost as unsteady as hers.

Clutching the sleeve of his sweatshirt, she said, "This is drenched, too." She fumbled for the zipper pull in the dark and tugged it down.

He shrugged out of it and let it fall to the floor.

She did the same with her sweater.

"Everything's wet," Dean said gruffly, running his hands over her hips, clad in sodden denim, and up the front of her damp shirt. He slid the top button through its hole.

Laura unbuttoned his shirt as he unbuttoned hers, working quickly, awkwardly, their breathing far too loud in the nighttime quiet of the house. She got his shirt open first, and yanked it over his shoulders. He flung it to the ground and tore at hers; something gave, and suddenly it wasn't on her anymore.

She quivered as he skimmed his hands hotly up her arms, across her shoulders and down over her breasts, still covered by the ribbed cotton tank top she wore in lieu of a bra. He unsnapped and unzipped her wet jeans, shoved them down over her panties. Kicking them aside, she reached for his fly, felt how hard he was, how ready, and flicked open the snap.

Dean closed a tremulous hand over hers as she began to lower the zipper. "Laura...honey..." He burrowed his other hand into her rain-dampened hair, kissed her forehead. "Let's go upstairs."

She shook her head. "We might wake Janey—she was restless. Here..." Taking him by the hand, she led him to the moonlit living room and Grandma Jane's lumpy old afghan-covered couch, which she had refused to replace with the Italian leather sofa Dean bought her. "Is this all right, or—"

He kissed her, his hands wrapped around her head, his body pressing against her, so warm, so hard....

She couldn't breathe, couldn't think, her heart pounding so wildly she thought it might explode.

His hands were everywhere on her, restless, needful. He tugged her tank top over her head. She clawed at his jeans, pulled him to her in a fever of need.

The world spun crazily, and then the couch was beneath her and he was on top of her, tearing her panties off, all heat and urgency now, and then he was—

"Oh..."

—pressing into her, stretching her open as he filled her...

"Wait. Dean, wait. We need...do you have...?"

His chest pumping, he stilled, half-buried within her. "Yes," he breathed shakily, dropping his forehead to hers. "Sorry. I'm too...in too much of a hurry."

He kissed her gently, withdrew, felt around on the floor for his jeans. Laura heard the crackle of plastic, and moments later she was in his arms again, skin against skin, need meeting need....

He drove into her hard, a burning lunge that forced a little whimper from her.

"Laura? Are you...did I...?"

"A little slower," she whispered, gathering him close. "It's been...a long time. Six years."

"Oh, honey..." He kissed her, tenderly this time, his hands tangled in her hair, his body rocking into hers slowly, slowly....

By the time he was fully inside her, she was quivering on the edge. He kept her there for a delirious eternity, making slow, mesmerizing love to her, the couch springs grating with every sinuous thrust. They kissed and stroked each other as their bodies shifted and slid together, a dance of the senses that grew inexorably swifter, more frenzied, until it consumed them both, together, in a single convulsive burst of pleasure.

12

"I WAS SO CRAZY about you," Dean murmured into Laura's ear as they lay snuggled together under Grandma Jane's pink wool afghan, her old fringed velvet throw pillow beneath their heads. Laura had torn the afghan off the back of the couch at the end, he'd told her as they lay together afterward, damp and trembling and still intimately joined; but she couldn't recall having done that. She hadn't been aware of anything but pleasure—astonishing, heart-stopping pleasure—and the bone-deep gratification of sharing it with Dean, after all these years.

"I was," he continued softly, nuzzling her hair, his arms and legs tangled companionably with hers. "I was out of my mind, back at Rutgers. It was like this...*pain*, this hurt, every time I looked at you...and yet there was also this amazing *joy*, this thrill that filled me whenever we were in the same room."

She turned to look at him, his eyes luminous in the dark, and so achingly sincere.

"I knew you loved Will," he said, brushing her hair, damp with rain and sweat, off her face. "I wanted you to feel that way about me. I wanted you to feel what I felt." He paused for a moment, took a breath. "I loved you, Laura."

She closed her eyes, wanting to say it, to share what

had been in her heart then and lingered still, but not trusting her own instincts in this charged and breathless moment.

He seemed to understand; she felt his lips, warm and tender, on her forehead. Quietly he said, "You were afraid of me. I knew that. And then there was Will. I wouldn't have done anything to hurt him, and neither would you—especially not you. Knowing you, you would have belted me one if I'd...you know."

She said, "If you'd just, like, come on to me, tried to coax me into the sack like you were always doing with girls, yeah, probably. But not if you'd taken me aside and...told me how you felt. We could have talked about it, cleared the air. Maybe we should have."

He shook his head. "That would have a huge mistake, messed everything up. There were the three of us, you know, and...I mean, I was in agony from wanting you, but at least it was my own business, my own shameful little secret, being stuck on my best friend's girl. If I'd told you, everything would have gotten all *awkward*, you know? And you would have ended up pitying me, and I don't think I could have taken that."

"I wouldn't have pitied you." Not much—not any more than she had pitied herself.

He shifted a bit, tucking her head under his chin. "At the time, I told myself it was for the best. You and I were such complete opposites. I mean, you were— you *are*—the kind of woman a man starts making plans about, the kind that makes him think about settling down. If he's the settling-down type."

"Which you've never been."

He didn't respond to that. From the tension in his arms, she sensed a pensiveness, an uncertainty.

"I remember how you used to go on about marriage," she said. "All that ranting about how it was the husbands who were the indentured servants, not the wives. You used to say marriage was the biggest scam ever perpetrated under the guise of 'civilization.'"

"I used to say a lot of stupid things." The statement might have come off as glib had there been a speck of amusement in his voice. "I knew I was lousy husband material. That's why I used to say those things."

"Ah, the Dean-Kettering-as-screwup theory," she said, trying to lighten things up.

"I wish it was just a theory," he said gravely. "But judging from my own past behavior, and keeping in mind that there might actually be something to genetics..."

"I'll accept that you've never been a Boy Scout," she said, "but please spare me the comparisons between you and your father. I'm not buying that voodoo—I never have. You are who you are. If you've made some mistakes..."

"I've made some whoppers, as you're all too aware. I've hurt people. I hurt *you*—inexcusably—when I walked out on you six years ago without so much as saying goodbye. You must have hated me. I guess you did, since you never got in touch with me, and I can't blame—"

"But I did—or tried to. The air force wouldn't tell me where you were."

"They'd put me in a special intelligence unit, anti-terrorist stuff, real hush-hush." He moved so that he was looking into her eyes. "You seriously tried to find me? God, I would have thought you'd never want to hear from me again, after what I..." He shook his head. "Why did you?"

Ah, the sixty-four thousand dollar question. Why had she brought that up, about trying to find him? What had she been thinking of? "I...it doesn't matter why."

"It does to me," he said, pulling her closer. "It means I maybe didn't blow it as badly as I'd thought that night. It means you didn't despise me—or did you? You weren't trying to find me just to read me the riot act, were you?"

"No, no, it was nothing like that." Kay would tell her it was a Freudian slip, blurting that out about contacting the air force, that she subconsciously wanted Dean to know he was Janey's father. Was she wrong to persist in keeping it a secret? Did he have a right to know? At one time—when she'd first found out she was pregnant—she'd thought so, but then so many years had passed, years in which he'd gone his own way, lived his own life, a life that could never have accommodated a wife and child.

"Were you...did you think we actually had a chance together, you and me?" Dean asked, sounding almost hopeful. "Did you want to see if we could make it work? 'Cause that would have really made me happy, knowing you thought I could be redeemed, even if you were wrong."

She sighed. "It wasn't that. When I found you gone that morning, I knew there was no chance of...you and me."

"Yeah," he said shortly. "I knew I'd blown it."

"I just...I needed to...talk to you. There was...something I wanted to tell you, that's all."

"What?" he asked, his gaze so serious, so unsuspecting. "What did you want to tell me?"

Laura struggled, heart pounding, to think this through rationally. If she told him now, everything would change. He would be a part of their lives—of Janey's life—in a way that could never be taken back, never undone. Right now, basking in postcoital intimacy and contentment, with Dean opening his heart to her with such compelling candor, she ached to tell him.

But how would she feel tomorrow, in the merciless light of morning, with Dean counting down the days till he left Port Liv and sailed off to Bermuda?

"Laura?" Dean prompted.

This wasn't the right moment—not now, while she was so vulnerable, so distracted—to disclose what she'd kept so carefully hidden for so long. There would be plenty of time tomorrow, when they were apart and she could think clearly, to decide whether to tell him.

"I can't remember what it was," she said without looking at him, the lie imparting a thready, stilted quality to her voice. *The Laura I used to know could never have lied so baldly.* "It must not have been that important."

He nodded thoughtfully, gathered her more firmly in his arms. "It must have seemed important at the time."

"It was a long time ago," she said. "Nothing's the same as it was then."

"Some things haven't changed." He touched his lips gently to her eyelids, her cheek, her nose. "You're still the only one," he whispered against her lips as he trailed his fingers lightly down over her breast. "It was always you, always. You're the only woman I've ever loved, or ever will."

SHE WAS SLEEPING, he realized when he heard her steady breathing, felt her warm, somnolent weight against him.

The second time had been as impassioned as the first, but different. She had taken the reins, rolling on top of *him*, which was not only intensely arousing, but touching, because he knew why she was doing it; it had to do with his blaming himself for that night six years ago. *We were both responsible for that night*, she had told him. And now she wanted him to know that she was equally responsible for tonight. Should they find reasons tomorrow to regret making love, it would be on her head as well as his.

Would he regret it? he asked himself as he gazed at Laura's face in the dark.

No. Never. He'd just made love to the woman he loved—a woman who, unless he was completely delusional, was also in love with him, even if she couldn't acknowledge it yet. The past obstacle to that love—her relationship with Will—was no longer a factor. Will—sweet, good-natured Will, whom they had both adored—was gone. The pain of his death, which had been such a fresh, stinging wound six years ago, had dissipated with time until it was but a hint of sorrow underscoring the joy of having known him.

So, no. Dean did not regret this night, would never regret it.

Would Laura?

Her breath fluttered a few hairs that had fallen across her face; Dean smoothed them away cautiously, so as not to wake her.

Her regret six years ago had been a function of Dean's having abandoned her so abruptly and thoroughly. What if he didn't leave this time? What if he was here not only tomorrow morning when she woke up, but the next day, and the next, and the next?

What if...

His heart rattled in his chest. He could scarcely believe he was contemplating...what?

Commitment? Marriage?

Laura wouldn't go to Bermuda with him; she'd made that clear. What if he stayed here for the summer, took a stab at working it out with her?

Was he good enough for her? No. Even she seemed to know that, tonight notwithstanding.

Should that stop him? Maybe.

Maybe not.

Marrying Laura would mean becoming a stepfather to Janey. The thought filled him with a profound sense of rightness, tainted just slightly with fear. What if he turned out to be as lousy at family life as his old man? Was Laura right when she called his genetics theory voodoo, or had he actually known what he was talking about all these years? Was he prepared to shoulder the responsibility of taking care of a child?

He *had* put the wheels in motion to set up that trust fund; if that wasn't responsible, what was?

Thinking about the trust fund reminded him of Laura's opposition to it, as mystifying as her adamant unwillingness to accept the myriad guilt offerings he'd laid at her feet these past seven weeks. For her to stymie his efforts to create a nest egg for her daughter hinted at a deep, underlying wariness as regarded Dean.

Not that she didn't have reason to be wary, given his personal history. But it didn't set well with him that she should deny Janey this financial boon just because...because what?

Don't ask me to explain it....

And he'd promised her he wouldn't. But that didn't mean he had to deny Janey her trust fund. It just meant he'd have to come up with her birth certificate and Social Security number on his own.

With slow, careful movements, Dean extricated himself from Laura's sleeping embrace, tucked the afghan snugly around her and pulled on his jeans. *Okay, if I were a birth certificate, where would I be hiding?*

He scanned the living room in the dark, recreating its furnishings in his mind—couch, coffee table, chairs, TV, woodstove, a couple of lamps and end tables...nothing in which important papers might be secreted.

Walking silently on bare feet down the hall, he went into the kitchen and flipped the light switch, squinting as the overhead lamps snapped on. A quick rifle of the drawers and cabinets revealed nothing other than the usual kitchen stuff. His search of Laura's studio was just as fruitless. There was a big steel cabinet against one wall, but all it contained was art supplies.

Dean closed his eyes and rubbed the bridge of his nose. He seemed to recall having seen a desk somewhere in this house—one of those old-fashioned ones, with a top that rolled up and down.

"Yes," he whispered when it came to him. Retracing his steps down the hall, he took the stairs two at a time, wincing every time his foot landed on a creaky one. Groping on the wall of Laura's bedroom, he found a light switch and thumbed it. A floor lamp went on; he smiled when he saw that it was situated conveniently next to the rolltop desk in the corner.

Settling himself in the old swivel-seated desk chair, Dean raised the slatted rolltop and blinked at the Byzantine arrangement of slots and cubbyholes he encountered, most crammed with papers. He moved the lamp closer and set about removing, inspecting and replacing the contents of every nook and cranny: paid bills, unpaid bills, sales receipts for paintings, tax documentation, assorted business cards, correspondence, bank statements....

Ah. In a wide, shallow drawer near the bottom, he found a nine-by-twelve kraft envelope with "Janey" inked on it in whimsically ornate letters surrounded by a circle of cavorting monkeys. Smiling, he opened the clasp and slid the envelope's contents onto the bare desktop. On top was a little booklet that turned out to contain a record of Janey's vaccinations. Next came a handful of photographs.

The first was of Laura and Kay mugging in the front yard of Laura's house after what looked to have been a snowstorm of titanic proportions. Kay, wielding a hammer and chisel in that gaudy blanket coat of hers, and sporting a black beret and a painted-on mustache and goatee, was playing the part of a sculptor putting the finishing touches on a snowman. Oh. Not a snow-*man*, Dean saw—a snow*woman* patterned after those primitive fertility icons of women with pendulous breasts and gigantic pregnant bellies. Laura, looking about twelve months pregnant herself in an unzipped parka and maternity sweatsuit, stood a few feet away in the same posture as the snowwoman, as if posing for it.

Dean's chuckles ceased when he encountered the next picture, one of those grainy black-and-white ultrasound snapshots of an unborn baby—Janey, obviously. Sucking her thumb. His throat tightened as he gazed in wonderment at the sweet, fragile little baby girl curled up in her mother's womb.

The next snapshot made him smile again: Laura in a hospital bed, wearing one of those awful institutional cotton gowns, smiling down at the newborn daughter sleeping in her arms. No, not sleeping, Dean realized, but nursing. The gown had been pulled down to free one of Laura's arms and bare an astonishingly full and luxuriant breast. Janey, with that Sid Vicious hair and swaddled in a thin little blanket, was suckling with her eyes closed, one hand resting possessively on the creamy, blue-veined upper slope of the breast. In a corner of the snapshot Dean saw one of those little rolling tables bearing a tray of food, half-eaten, and next to it, a paper napkin with a drawing of Janey on it—the same drawing that now hung in Laura's studio, framed like the most priceless artwork.

In an envelope beneath the photographs, Dean struck pay dirt in the form of Janey's Social Security card. "Yes!" Poking around for something to write on, he found a legal pad and pen, copied down the number, folded up the sheet and stuck it in his back pocket.

The next item was a folded-up sheet of drawing paper. He assumed it was another sketch of Janey until he opened it and, with a dull jolt of recognition, saw the border of teddy bears and rattles that surrounded Laura's final letter to Will.... "Remember that night we decided to throw away my diaphragm?"

Dean put the letter down, scrubbed his hands over his face...

He picked it up again and skimmed it, reliving the sick tide of comprehension that had gripped him at the revelation of Laura's pregnancy. "Yes, I'm sure it's for real.... I'm only four or five weeks along right now, but I've got a due date! October 7—your sister Bridget's birthday...."

Dean read that last line again. "October 7—your sister Bridget's birthday."

October 7.

Frowning, he sorted through the snapshots until he came to the first one, the comical tableau of Laura posing as the archetypal fertility symbol for Kay. The snow was a foot thick where it hadn't been shoveled, deeper where it had drifted. It was unequivocally a winter scene, taken no earlier than mid-November at the outside, although Long Island usually didn't see snow like that until much further into the season.

Focusing on the image of Laura, big with child—
huge with child—Dean had to figure she was almost
due, if not overdue. Yet she'd been given a due date of
October 7, and this picture had to have been taken
well after that.

It didn't make sense. Unless Janey had already been
born and, in the interest of humor, Laura had stuffed
her sweatshirt with pillows for the camera.

That was it. That had to be it. Dean was certain of it.

Then why were his hands trembling?

Shoving aside what he'd looked at already, Dean
rummaged swiftly through the remaining "Janey"
items until he came to a six-by-nine envelope addressed to Laura from the Suffolk County Health De-
partment and bearing the legend Do Not Fold Or
Bend in big black letters. Reaching into the end that
had been ripped open, he slid out a pale green document with Certificate of Birth Registration printed in
an officious gothic typeface across the top. "This cer-
tifies that a certificate of birth has been filed under the
name of: Jane Bridget Sweeney. Sex: Female. Born
on..."

"January 1?" Dean whispered incredulously.

"At: Stony Brook, New York. Name of father..."

That space was blank.

Dean stared at the certificate, but it was shaking too
badly to read.

It was his hand that was shaking, along with the rest
of him. He dropped the certificate onto the desk.
Pushed his chair back. Sat there, gazing at the blank
space on Janey's birth certificate.

The blank space where Will Sweeney's name

should have been. He raked both palsied hands through his hair, startled to find there was almost none left. Oh, yeah...*Wanna play barbershop, Mr. Kettlewing?*

"My God..." Could it be?

Frantically he sorted through the papers on the desk until he located the letter to Will, which was dated February 3. *I went to Dr. Chang this morning. She says I'm only four or five weeks along right now....*

How, if Laura had gotten pregnant by Will around the beginning of '95, could she have gotten pregnant again by Dean four months later? Unless...

Yes. She must have lost the baby, the first baby, Will's baby. She must have miscarried sometime after Will's death but before Dean's visit in April.

"Oh, Laura, Laura..." Leaning his elbows on the desk, Dean dropped his face in his hands. First she'd had to endure the news about Will, then a miscarriage, and then...

In his mind's eye, he saw himself throwing her onto her bed, tearing at her nightgown, ramming into her....

We were both responsible for that night.

Even if that were true, and it wasn't, not really, they both knew who was responsible for her waking up the next morning alone, bewildered, remorseful. And then, a few weeks later, when she discovered she was pregnant again...

The air force wouldn't tell me where you were.... There was something I wanted to tell you.

He knew now what that was. But when he'd asked

her about it, not an hour ago, she'd told him she couldn't remember, that it wasn't important.

She'd lied. He'd heard it in her voice, the telltale strain, but he'd dismissed it from his mind. But he should have known. She'd never been able to lie worth a damn. The only time she could ever bring herself to do it was when the alternative was so distasteful that there was essentially no other choice.

In the beginning, she'd wanted to tell him, but then she'd changed her mind when she'd thought about what it would mean to acknowledge someone like him as the father of her child. She'd wised up.

But then, she'd always been pretty levelheaded.

"God..." Dean lifted the ultrasound picture of Janey. His breath snagged in his throat, stinging his eyes. He brushed his thumb over the picture, as if trying to touch the spidery fingers, the unformed face—the face of his daughter. The knowledge that he had a child, and that that child was Janey, was both humbling and exhilarating. The knowledge that Laura was desperate to keep the truth from him, even now, after tonight...

She may have wanted to sleep with him, she might even love him. But she knew better than to try and make a life with him.

He flung the picture down, ground the heels of his hands against his forehead. This was why Laura wouldn't take his money or his gifts, or let him start a trust fund for Janey. She would have felt honor bound to tell him the truth then, and that would have meant letting him back into her life, into Janey's life, something she was obviously determined not to do.

Could he blame her, with his track record? She knew him better than anyone; she knew he wasn't the type to turn over a new leaf, regardless of his pipe dreams. Had he really been contemplating marriage tonight?

Bitter laughter shook his chest. Yeah, right. A few weeks of domestic tranquility and suddenly he was *Father Knows Best*. How long would that have lasted?

It was his own damn fault, this whole hopeless fiasco—but what else was new?

While gathering up the pictures and documents, Dean came across several photocopies of the birth certificate paper-clipped together. He folded up one and tucked it in his pocket, set the original certificate aside and returned everything else to the envelope marked "Janey."

Then he reached once more for the legal pad and pen.

13

"MOMMY? You cwyin'?"

Laura looked up from where she sat on the edge of her bed in her chenille robe, to find Janey standing in the doorway, having obviously just tumbled out of her own bed.

"No, sweetie," Laura said in a wet, scratchy voice. "I'm fine." Not strictly a lie, since her tears had mostly subsided, although she must be a puffy, red-faced mess for Janey to have asked the question.

Padding into the bedroom in her sleep-rumpled dinosaur jammies, her hair a flaxen snarl, Janey eyed the legal pad in Laura's hand. "What's that?"

"Nothing." *Liar.* If it was nothing, then why had Laura collapsed in tears when she came up here this morning, after awakening on the living room couch, and discovered it on her desk?

Next to—God help her—Janey's birth certificate.

"Whatsa matter, Mommy?" Janey asked in that very grown-up, tell-me-all-about-it voice she'd probably picked up from her aunt Kay. Climbing up onto the bed, she put her arms around Laura and squeezed. "It can't be that bad."

Her despair notwithstanding, Laura couldn't suppress a raspy little chuckle as she returned Janey's hug and kissed her tousled hair. "You're a great kid, you know that, monkey?"

Janey smiled impishly. "That's what you're always telling me." Her gaze lit on the legal pad, the top sheet of which was covered with Dean's unique, angular handwriting. "Is that from Mr. Kettle-wing?"

"How did you know that?"

"He wites like that—like he's mad about something. Only he's never mad about anything. He's the *coolest*."

"Yeah, he's pretty cool," Laura muttered, rubbing her forehead. *Don't do it. Don't break down in front of Janey. Suck it up.*

"Will you wead it to me?" Janey asked, snuggling up against her mom.

"No, monkey. It's...personal. He wrote it to me."

With a little huff of displeasure, Janey said, "I'll just ask *him* what it says."

Oh, God. "Janey...sweetie. You can't do that. Mr. Kettering...he's gone. He left. He went b-back to—" Laura bit her bottom lip to stop it from quivering "—Portsmouth. Where his boat is—where he lives."

"But..." Distress contorted Janey's face. "I thought he was gonna stay till Aunt Kay got back."

"So did I, sweetie, but...he decided to go back early."

"Why?"

"I..." Laura's gaze dropped to the legal pad. "It's complicated."

"He didn't say goodbye to me." Janey's eyes were filling with tears, her face crumpling. "Why didn't he say goodbye to me?"

"In the note, he asked me to say goodbye to you for him."

"It's not the same thing," Janey whimpered, curling up into a ball and sliding her thumb into her mouth. It was the first time in months she'd surrendered to the urge to suck her thumb, yet she didn't even seem aware she was doing it.

"Oh, sweetie..." Laura tucked Janey firmly into her embrace, using the sash of her robe to dry the child's tears. "I know he felt real bad, not being able to say it in person. Do you want me to read that part of the note to you?"

Janey extracted the thumb just long enough to say, "I want you to wead the whole thing. I want to know why he left."

Although she'd read the note half a dozen times, Laura skimmed it again, keeping in mind Janey's five-year-old sensibilities and how much she knew—and didn't know—about her mother and "Mr. Kettle-wing." But keeping in mind, as well, Laura's personal mandate to be as frank and honest with everyone—especially her own child—as she could.

"Okay, Janey, tell you what. I'll read you the note—most of it. The really personal parts I'll skip over. But if there's anything in the note you don't understand—and there will be—I want you to promise to ask me about it afterward. How about that?"

Janey ruminated on that in thumb-sucking silence for a moment, then nodded.

"Okay." Drawing in a deep, steadying breath, Laura started to read from the note. "'Dear Laura. This is the hardest thing I've ever done, leaving you like this. I know it's going to feel the same to you as it did six years ago, but—'"

Out popped the thumb. "What happened six years ago?"

"Wait till I'm done, sweetie, and then I'll answer all your questions." Laura cautioned herself to be a little more circumspect about which parts she read out loud. "Okay, let's see...I think I can skip this next part." The part about how this time it was different because he'd actually been thinking about proposing to her before he found Janey's birth certificate and sorted out the truth—and realized that Laura would never, in a million years, let him play that fundamental role in her life, and especially not in Janey's. He hastened to explain that, as painful as this was to him, he understood and even appreciated the wisdom of it.

"Mommy, wead it," Janey said plaintively around the thumb.

"Uh..." This next bit should be all right, Laura decided. "'The weeks I spent with you and Janey kind of got to me, I guess. They made me feel like I could maybe be a different kind of man, someone who could be part of a family and like it. But it was all just smoke and mirrors.'"

"Smoke and what?"

"Make believe. 'You're right about me, Lorelei. You've always had my number. Some dogs can't be trained.'"

Janey frowned as she gnawed on the thumb. "What dog?"

"No, sweetie, it's a metaphor—a way of saying

something by drawing a comparison to something else."

Janey gave her one those "Say what?" looks.

"He means he's not the kind of man who can change."

"That's *stoopit!*" Janey looked down at her wet thumb as if noticing it for the first time, and wiped it on her pajamas. "He can so change."

"Sweetie, I think he might just have a point. Some people have a lot of trouble changing."

"Not Mr. Kettle-wing. He smoked cigawettes when he came here, wemember? But he stopped wight away and never started again."

"Um, yeah, and that's good. That's great. Smoking is really bad for you. But I don't think that's the kind of changing he's talking about."

"He let me cut his hair."

Laura sighed. "Again, that's...you know...just how he *looks*. It doesn't really have anything to do with who he is inside."

"Yes, it does, 'cause when he first came here, he was all, like...closed up inside himself." Janey illustrated this observation by going fetal again, her arms tightly wrapped around her legs, her head tucked in. "But lately he's been, like..." Unfolding her little body, she sprawled out on the bed with a goofy smile on her face.

Laura smiled when she remembered how Dean had looked last night while Janey was cutting his hair—the indolent pose, the blissed-out grin—and realized Janey had a point.

Sitting up and leaning over the legal pad, Janey asked, "What else does he say?"

"Let's see..." Laura found her place in the note. Dean had switched gears to tell her that he'd spent only about $120,000 of the million—*only?*—and that the remainder was in a joint account under both their names, so she could access it as needed. Anything that was left when he returned from Bermuda would go into Janey's trust fund, which he still intended to establish.

"Mommy," Janey pressed. "Wead it!"

"Ah, here we go. 'Tell Kay I'm sorry to drop the ball like this, after promising her I'd look after the Blue Mist and take reservations and all that while she was gone. I guess you'll have to do it. I can't tell you how bad I feel about leaving in the middle of the night this way, especially after...' Hmm..." Laura skipped over the reprise of his having done the same thing six years ago. "'The thing is, I just couldn't bear to say goodbye to you in person, or Janey, either, knowing I might...'" Laura's breath hitched. She reread the next few lines silently to herself. *...knowing I might never see either one of you again. I can't think about that, or I'll never have the courage to drive away. I meant it when I said this is the hardest thing I've ever done.*

"Mommeee."

"'So you'll have to say goodbye to Janey for me. Tell her I think she's the greatest—smart and creative and with both feet on the ground, just like her mom. I'm so proud of her—and of you, for being such an incredible mother and helping her to grow up so great. I'm glad she takes after you and n-not—'" Laura drew in a ragged breath as she skipped over that bit. "'If it's okay with you, I'd like you to tell Janey how much I l-love...'" Hot tears spilled from Laura's eyes; she dropped the pad onto her lap and buried her face in her hands, shoulders convulsing.

"That's okay, Mommy," Janey said consolingly, patting her on the back as she wept. "You don't have to wead any more."

Through an effort of will, Laura pulled herself together. "I'm sorry, sweetie. I hate for you to see me this way. I'm just..." She shook her head helplessly.

"You're sad that he's gone," Janey said. "Me, too."

Laura snatched a tissue out of the box on the night table and blew her nose.

"But he's not like those dogs, though," Janey said.

"What?"

"Those dogs that can't be twained. He's like the dinosaurs in the Cwetaceous pewiod."

Laura cocked her head. "The dinosaurs in the Cretaceous period."

"The ones that turned into birds. Maybe some of them don't *know* they turned into birds. Maybe they still think they're dinosaurs."

"Uh..."

"It's a metaphor," Janey said, with that look of exaggerated patience she adopted whenever it fell to her to illuminate dim-witted grown-ups.

Laura smiled. "I think I get it. So Mr. Kettering has gone and sprouted wings, but he just doesn't realize it yet?"

Janey nodded. "Why else would he wite such a nice note?"

Laura stared at the legal pad in her hands, a sense of epiphany glowing within her, like the sun coming out from the clouds. Why, indeed, would he write such a nice note?

Why would he write a note at all?

"Mommy? What's so funny?"

"What? Oh—nothing."

"You were smiling like something was funny."

"Not funny, just..." Laura filled her lungs with air and let it out. She looked from her daughter to the note written by the man who had fathered her. *I'd like you to tell Janey how much I love her. And if you decide to tell her—I mean, you wouldn't, I know that, but if you decide to tell her everything, that would be okay with me. More than okay. It would be great.*

What had Kay said? *If you explain it right, she'll understand.*

"Hey, monkey?" Laura said, wrapping an arm around Janey and pulling her close. "I've got something to tell you—something pretty huge."

"DEAN KETTERING?" The old salt who looked like Popeye, but whose name had actually turned out to be Ernie, scrunched one eye shut against the afternoon sun beating down on Howell's Marina and peered at Laura out of the other. "He's gone."

"Oh, no...I *knew* it." This was what Laura had most feared, that she wouldn't make it up to Portsmouth before Dean left. She'd had to put this trip off until Kay returned from vacation yesterday so that there would be someone to look after Janey while she was gone. She had been tempted to bring Janey along, but vetoed the idea, not wanting to inject a five-year-old into such a delicate situation.

If only Dean had a phone, she could have called him days ago.

"Yup." Popeye plucked his pipe out of his mouth to take a gulp from his coffee cup, which, judging from the smell on his breath, did not contain coffee. "Kettering was gone for almost two months there. Then he come back with one of them gay haircuts—I didn't ask no questions—and he starts workin' like a demon, fixin' up the *Lorelei* and layin' in food and water and fuel and whatnot. He had a bug up his ass, all right— paid me to help him get ready so's it'd go quicker, and he's the type likes to make do by himself. I bought him—let's see—sixty-one gallons of diesel, six gallons of kerosene, two cans of propane—"

"Thank you, Ernie," Laura said morosely. "I get the idea. When did he leave?"

"Let's see...that would have to have been last Wednesday. Wednesday, May twenty-third."

"Five days ago," Laura murmured. "He said it would take him about a week to sail to Bermuda."

"Well, that's countin' on fair weather," Ernie said. "My guess is it's gonna take him longer'n that, what with those storms they been havin' out in the Atlantic."

"Storms?"

"They were reportin' a Force 8 gale with twelve-foot seas yesterday. At least one boat's gone down already, is what I hear. I *told* Kettering it was a mite too early to be headin' out. I told him he should wait at least another week or two, but he was all fired up to get goin'." Ernie shook his head mournfully as he took another swallow. "If you're the prayin' kind, I'd do some prayin' for your friend there."

"I am, and I will," Laura said. And that wasn't all she would do. "Um...listen, do you mind my asking where you got that coffee cup?"

"Like it, do ya?" Ernie held up the thick stoneware mug to admire the Yankee whaler emblazoned on it above the legend World's Greatest Dad. "Happens I was haulin' them cans of propane up onto the *Lorelei* when I seen Kettering throw this here mug into a box of trash he was fixin' to heave. I fished it out and saw it was cracked, but he said it didn't leak none. Said I could have it if I wanted, so I took it. Them was fine boats, them whalers."

"Did he tell you why he was throwing it out?"

"Said he just didn't want it on the boat no more." Ernie lifted his shoulders in a "go-figure" shrug. "Said he liked it well enough when he bought it, but now he just can't stand the sight of it."

14

"THOSE OF YOU SEATED on the righthand side of the airplane," the pilot announced in his good-old-boy pilot's voice, "will have a pretty fair view of Bermuda coming up soon."

Breathe in, breathe out, Laura chanted to herself as she concentrated on staring fixedly at the seat in front of her.

"It's okay, Mommy," Janey soothed as she pried Laura's rigid fingers off their shared armrest and wrapped her cool little hands around them. "They said we'll be landing soon."

Landings and takeoffs, Laura thought, *that's where all the crashes happen.*

"Look!" Reaching across her, Janey pointed out the window next to Laura. "There it is!"

"I don't want to look," Laura said woodenly.

"But it's so pwetty! Mommy, please look."

Be strong for Janey. Don't let her think her mom's a world-class wuss, even if she is. Swallowing down the fear roiling in her stomach, Laura turned her head stiffly to look out the window. "Oh."

Far below, resembling a blue-green jewel surrounded by the vast and shimmering Atlantic, was the cluster of coral islands that made up Bermuda. This bird's-eye view drove home how small and remote

Bermuda was. Sailors had to navigate hundreds of miles of ocean to find it. Only the most dauntless among them—like Dean—embraced the challenge.

Upon arriving home Tuesday from her fruitless trip to Portsmouth, Laura had called a travel agent and booked two round-trip tickets on the first available flight to Bermuda, paid for by tapping into the joint bank account Dean had mentioned in his note. Janey had been more than happy to miss two weeks of pre-school for the opportunity to see "Mr. Kettle-wing" again; that she would be visiting a new and exotic locale had not seemed to impress her in the least.

Laura studied the close-set islands as the plane descended, making out scatterings of white rooftops shielded by tall palms. She could see cruise ships docked at the Royal Naval Dockyard, the city of Hamilton and the town of Saint George, although she knew from what Kay had gleaned off the Internet that Saint George's Harbour was the only permissible point of entry for private boats like Dean's.

Today was the first of June, which meant that nine days had passed since Dean had sailed out of Portsmouth—and into Force 8 gales. Assuming he had weathered the storms and made it safely to Bermuda, he should be easy enough to find. Boats just arriving in Saint George's Harbour had to obtain clearance at the customs dock on Ordnance Island, an islet connected by a walkway to the town of Saint George. Afterward, sailors living aboard their boats anchored them off the north side of Ordnance Island. If the *Lorelei* wasn't there, Laura would assume the storms had merely thrown Dean off schedule, and that he would be along in a day or two; any other possibility didn't bear thinking about.

For now, she would expect to find the *Lorelei* resting safely at anchor off Ordnance Island when she got there. She had enough to worry about, what with this plane about to—

A series of hard thuds jolted Laura out of her reverie. She yelped—*Omigod, we really are crashing!*—only to feel Janey's little hand giving hers a reassuring squeeze. "That was just the wheels hitting the gwound, Mommy. We've landed."

Laura slumped back in her seat, expelling a sigh of profound relief. They'd landed. It was over.

That wasn't so bad, she thought, breathing deeply of the balmy, sweet-scented air as she ushered Janey down the stairway that had been rolled up to the door of the plane. It would have been about a thousand times easier if she'd just kicked back and not listened to every little sound the plane made, speculating on imminent disaster. She promised herself she'd do it right on the flight back. She'd play the grown-up instead of leaving that role to a five-year-old.

Following the other passengers and the signs, Laura led Janey across the tarmac and into the terminal, where it didn't take long at all to be processed through the "Arrival Hall," collecting their luggage and passing through customs. Outside, she commandeered a taxi driven by an amiable fellow in shorts and knee socks appropriately named Gaby, who held forth on the flora, fauna and geography of Bermuda while transporting them to their lodgings.

Laura had chosen their guest house, a charming little place ringed with verandas and nestled among drifts of hibiscus, oleander and Japanese pines, for its location overlooking Saint George. After checking into their room and changing into shorts and T-shirts, Laura and Janey made their way into town via narrow lanes lined with white-roofed homes painted butter yellow, periwinkle, shell pink....

"Ooh, Mommy, do you hear that sound like thousands of little glass bells?" Janey asked excitedly. "Gaby said it's twee fwogs that make that sound! Can we twy and see one?"

"Not right now, monkey. We didn't come here to find tree frogs, you know."

"I know! We came here to find my daddy!"

My daddy... "Please be here, Dean," Laura whispered under her breath. "And please, *please* want *us* to be here."

She steered Janey into Saint George's quaintly archaic downtown district, which surrounded a bustling central area known as King's Square. Here, the locals were outnumbered by the tourists, several of whom were posing for snapshots with the antiquated stocks, pillory and whipping post at the north end of the square.

"What are those?" Laura asked, pointing to the heavy wooden contraptions.

"Um...those are old-fashioned instruments of punishment, sweetie. That one's called the stocks. People who did bad things would have their arms and hands locked into—"

"Let me see!" Janey pulled frantically on Laura's hand.

"Later. We're trying to find Mr. Ket—your daddy, remember? That's where we need to go," Laura said, pointing. "Ordnance Island."

In addition to the customs facility and cruise ship terminal, the little islet turned out to be home to a replica of a seventeenth-century sailing ship, which Janey stared at in evident fascination. Scrutinizing the anchorage off the islet's north side, Laura counted ten boats of various types, three of which looked to have incurred severe storm damage.

The *Lorelei* was not among them.

"Is he here, Mommy?"

Laura sighed. "Let's check the customs dock. Maybe he just got in."

He hadn't.

"Mommy, where is he? You said he was gonna be here."

"I know, sweetie." Feigning a nonchalance she didn't feel, Laura said, "He's just a little late—you know, like you're always late for preschool? No big deal. Let's go get some lunch. I'm starving."

"Can we look at that old boat first?"

"We sure can."

They explored the replica for almost an hour—Laura couldn't tear Janey away from it—then ate a lunch of spicy fish soup at a tavern overlooking the harbor. During another futile trip to the customs dock, Laura realized her anxiety was starting to rub off on Janey. They both needed to get their minds off Dean's absence, if only for a while.

Map in hand, Laura guided her daughter back through King's Square—where Janey gaped at the stocks and pillory, still occupied by tourists—and north by foot along meandering roads to Fort Saint Catherine. They explored the four-hundred-year-old stone keep and battlements for most of the afternoon. By the time they'd walked back into Saint George, they were both hot and exhausted.

"Look, Mommy!" Janey exclaimed as she dragged her mother by the hand through the tourists milling in King's Square. "Nobody's in the stocks. I can twy it out now."

"I don't know, sweetie." Laura cast an uneasy glance toward the sky, which was rapidly filling up with dense gray clouds. "It looks like it's gonna start pouring any second. We should really check Ordnance Island first in case—"

"Just for a minute?" Janey begged, pulling on Laura's hand. "I'll be quick, I promise."

"Okay, monkey—just for a minute."

The stocks, built onto a raised platform, had been constructed with a bench facing a wall of wooden panels that could slide up and down to secure a prisoner's hands and feet into appropriately sized holes. Since it had been designed with adult malefactors in mind, Janey was too small, when sitting on the bench, for her hands and feet to reach the holes. Her solution was to stand facing the wall and stick her hands through the top pair of holes.

"Look at me!" she squealed. "I'm a cwiminal!"

"That's great, sweetie," Laura said, wishing she'd thought to pack a camera. "You look really...uh-oh."

"What?"

"Feel that? It's starting to rain." Just random droplets right now, but it wouldn't stay that way. The other sightseers were already starting to scatter to the edges of King's Square. "Come on, sweetie, let's..."

Laura stilled, her gaze drawn to a tall man in a baseball cap and sunglasses standing on the other side of the square, in front of the Town Hall, motionless amid the tourists swarming around him. He reached up to pull off the shades just as the skies opened up.

"Mommy!" Janey shrieked.

Turning, Laura saw her daughter standing at the edge of the platform, arms outstretched, panicked from the sudden onslaught of rain. "It's okay, sweetie." Lifting the child down, Laura grabbed her hand and sprinted with her toward a nearby building whose second-floor veranda produced a sort of ground-level portico, beneath which about a dozen others had already gathered.

In the few seconds it took for Laura to hustle Janey to shelter, they were both soaked through from the driving rain. It swept in sheets across King's Square, now empty except for the last few stragglers seeking a haven from the deluge.

Was it Dean? Laura wondered as she gazed through the curtain of rain toward the spot where she'd seen the man in sunglasses. Had he seen her?

Janey tugged on her hand. "Whatsa matter, Mommy?" she asked over the dull drumming of the rain.

"Nothing, sweetie. I just...I thought I saw..."

A middle-aged couple in matching plaid shirts darted under the portico, nudging Laura and Janey back into the crowd and cutting off Laura's view of the square.

"'Scuse me." Still gripping Janey's hand, Laura muscled her way to the front again, even though it meant being more exposed to the rain. "'Scuse me."

"Mommy, is something wong?"

"No. Yes. I don't know. I think I'm seeing things. It's just…" Laura raked a hand through her sodden hair as she stared out at the rain-bleared Town Hall. Her throat felt clogged; she admonished herself not to cry in front of Janey, not again. "It's just so *maddening* not knowing whether he's here yet, if he made it through the storms okay, or…or…"

Janey squeezed her hand. "I'm sowwy I made us stop so I could twy out the stocks. You were wight. We should have looked for him first."

"Oh, sweetie." Turning to her daughter, Laura squatted down and took her in her arms. The crowd shifted, jostling them. Laura ignored the distraction as she blinked back impending tears. "You have no reason to be sorry. You didn't do anything wrong. We can come back tomorrow to look for him."

She gave Janey a consoling hug, thinking, *God, please let him be here by then. Please let him be okay. If anything's happened to him…*

"Laura?" A man's quiet, incredulous voice came from behind her.

Dean.

Laura spun around as she bolted to her feet. She breathed his name, reached for him.

"Oh, my God—Laura!" Dean whipped off his cap, gathered her up and kissed her, long and hard, his arms banded tightly around her, his hands gripping her almost painfully.

Over the murmurs and chuckles of the people around them, Laura heard Janey gasp and then let loose with a shrill, delighted little burst of laughter.

Dean clutched the back of her head, prolonging the kiss, deepening it. Drunk with joy, weak with relief, Laura returned it with equal fervor, thrilling to the warmth of him through his sodden clothes.

Janey yanked on Laura's T-shirt. "Mommy, everybody's looking."

That prompted a ripple of laughter from the crowd. Opening her eyes as the kiss gradually ebbed, Laura saw that the people huddled under the portico with them, having backed away to give them room, were watching the ardent reunion like it was television.

Dean wiped his thumbs gently over her cheeks; only then did she realize she was crying. With astonishment she saw that his eyes were shimmering, too. "Laura," he whispered. "God, I can't believe it's you." Looking down, he smiled and brushed a hand over Janey's damp hair. "Hey, monkey."

"You kissed my mommy!" Janey giggled.

"Yeah, and I think I'm gonna kiss her again."

He did, more softly this time, but with just as much lingering passion. By the time they drew apart, the rain had tapered off almost completely and the tourists sharing the portico with them were venturing out into King's Square once more.

"Quick rainstorm," Laura observed.

Dean nodded. "That's typical for Bermuda. It'll be nice now for the rest of the day."

"Dean, what happened to you?" Laura asked when she noticed the scabbed-over cut on his forehead, the contusion on the side of his jaw.

"Ran into a little drama on the high seas. Threw me off schedule—I only made it in a couple of hours ago. The *Lorelei*'s gonna need a little work, but it could have been a lot worse."

"I heard about those storms," she said, lightly touching his bruised jaw. "I was so upset when we got here and didn't see your boat."

"She was," Janey concurred. "She twied to act all cool, but she didn't fool me."

"I'm sorry you were worried." Dean captured her hand in his and kissed it. "Laura, honey..." He stroked her hair, her face, as if he still couldn't believe she was standing in front of him. "What are you doing here?"

Before Laura could phrase a response, Janey piped up with, "We came to ask you to mawwy us!"

"Janey!" Laura laughingly scolded as heat rose up her throat.

"Really?" Dean buried his hands in Laura's hair, searching her eyes. "Seriously? You...you want to..."

"I love you, Dean," Laura said quietly. "I do. I always have. I'm sorry I...couldn't say it before. I didn't have enough faith in you."

"I haven't done much to earn it."

"Yes, you have." She rested a hand on his cheek, raspy with a couple of days' worth of stubble. "I just wasn't paying enough attention."

"Well, you're making up for it now," he said. "Holy cow, did you actually *fly* here? You must have."

"She was vewy bwave," Janey said.

"I'll bet she was," Dean said, touching his lips to hers. "I love you, too, honey. I'm so glad you're here. I couldn't believe it when I saw you. I thought I must have hurt my head worse than I thought."

"Mommy says I don't have to call you Mr. Kettlewing anymore," Janey said. "She says I can call you Daddy, 'cause you really are my daddy—if it's okay with you."

Dean looked from Janey to Laura and back again, his eyes gleaming. "Oh, sweetie." Dropping to his knees, he folded Janey in his arms, squeezing his eyes shut. "It's a lot more than okay with me. It's..." When he opened his eyes, tears spilled from them. Meeting Laura's gaze, he mouthed, "Thank you."

Regaining his feet, he took Laura in his arms again and kissed her with heartbreaking tenderness.

"You guys," Janey said. "The wain has stopped."

So it had. Droplets still plopped onto the wet pavement from the roof above them, but there was nothing more coming out of the sky, and the few remaining clouds were retreating just as quickly as they'd appeared. King's Square was aswarm again with tourists, as if the fleeting cloudburst had never happened.

"Look at that," Laura marveled as they stepped out from under the portico into brilliant sunshine. "Just moments ago, it was rainy and dark and miserable, and now it's..."

"Perfect," Dean said, taking her hand and Janey's in his. "Absolutely perfect."

Pamela Burford presents

The Wedding Ring

*Four high school friends and a pact—
every girl gets her ideal mate by thirty or be
prepared for matchmaking! The rules are
simple. Give your "chosen" man three
months...and see what happens!*

Love's Funny That Way
Temptation #812—on sale December 2000
It's no joke when Raven Muldoon falls in love with comedy
club owner Hunter—*brother* of her "intended."

I Do, But Here's the Catch
Temptation #816—on sale January 2001
Charli Ross is more than willing to give up her status as
last of a dying breed—the thirty-year-old virgin—to Grant.
But all *he* wants is marriage.

One Eager Bride To Go
Temptation #820—on sale February 2001
Sunny Bleecker is still waiting tables at Wafflemania when
Kirk comes home from California and wants to marry her.
It's as if all her dreams have finally come true—except...

Fiancé for Hire
Temptation #824—on sale March 2001
No way is Amanda Coppersmith going to let
The Wedding Ring rope her into marriage. But no matter
how clever she is, Nick is one step ahead of her...

**"Pamela Burford creates the
memorable characters readers love!"**
—The Literary Times

Tyler Brides

It happened one weekend...

Quinn and Molly Spencer are delighted to accept three bookings for their newly opened B&B, Breakfast Inn Bed, located in America's favorite hometown, Tyler, Wisconsin.

But Gina Santori is anything but thrilled to discover her best friend has tricked her into sharing a room with the man who broke her heart eight years ago....

And Delia Mayhew can hardly believe that she's gotten herself locked in the Breakfast Inn Bed basement with the sexiest man in America.

Then there's Rebecca Salter. She's turned up at the Inn in her wedding gown. Minus her groom.

Come home to Tyler for three delightful novellas by three of your favorite authors: Kristine Rolofson, Heather MacAllister and Jacqueline Diamond.

HARLEQUIN®
Makes any time special ™

You're not going to believe this offer!

In October and November 2000, buy any two Harlequin or Silhouette books and save $10.00 off future purchases, or buy any three and save $20.00 off future purchases!

Just fill out this form and attach 2 proofs of purchase (cash register receipts) from October and November 2000 books and Harlequin will send you a coupon booklet worth a total savings of $10.00 off future purchases of Harlequin and Silhouette books in 2001. Send us 3 proofs of purchase and we will send you a coupon booklet worth a total savings of $20.00 off future purchases.

Saving money has never been this easy.

I accept your offer! Please send me a coupon booklet:

Name: _____

Address: _____ City: _____

State/Prov.: _____ Zip/Postal Code: _____

Optional Survey!

In a typical month, how many Harlequin or Silhouette books would you buy <u>new</u> at retail stores?

☐ Less than 1   ☐ 1   ☐ 2   ☐ 3 to 4   ☐ 5+

Which of the following statements best describes how you <u>buy</u> Harlequin or Silhouette books? Choose one answer only that <u>best</u> describes you.

☐ I am a regular buyer and reader
☐ I am a regular reader but buy only occasionally
☐ I only buy and read for specific times of the year, e.g. vacations
☐ I subscribe through Reader Service but also buy at retail stores
☐ I mainly borrow and buy only occasionally
☐ I am an occasional buyer and reader

Which of the following statements best describes how you <u>choose</u> the Harlequin and Silhouette series books you buy <u>new</u> at retail stores? By "series," we mean books within a particular line, such as *Harlequin PRESENTS* or *Silhouette SPECIAL EDITION*. Choose one answer only that <u>best</u> describes you.

☐ I only buy books from my favorite series
☐ I generally buy books from my favorite series but also buy books from other series on occasion
☐ I buy some books from my favorite series but also buy from many other series regularly
☐ I buy all types of books depending on my mood and what I find interesting and have no favorite series

Please send this form, along with your cash register receipts as proofs of purchase, to:
In the U.S.: Harlequin Books, P.O. Box 9057, Buffalo, NY 14269
In Canada: Harlequin Books, P.O. Box 622, Fort Erie, Ontario L2A 5X3
(Allow 4-6 weeks for delivery) Offer expires December 31, 2000.

PHQ4002

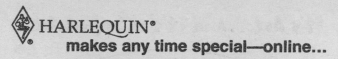

HARLEQUIN®

makes any time special—online...

eHARLEQUIN.com

shop eHarlequin

♥ Find all the new Harlequin releases at everyday great discounts.

♥ Try before you buy! Read an excerpt from the latest Harlequin novels.

♥ Write an online review and share your thoughts with others.

reading room

♥ Read our Internet exclusive daily and weekly online serials, or vote in our interactive novel.

♥ Talk to other readers about your favorite novels in our Reading Groups.

♥ Take our Choose-a-Book quiz to find the series that matches you!

authors' alcove

♥ Find out interesting tidbits and details about your favorite authors' lives, interests and writing habits.

♥ Ever dreamed of being an author? Enter our Writing Round Robin. The Winning Chapter will be published online! Or review our writing guidelines for submitting your novel.

It's hot...and it's out of control.

BLAZE

**This winter is going to be *hot, hot, hot!*
Don't miss these bold, provocative,
ultra-sexy books!**

SEDUCED by Janelle Denison
December 2000

Lawyer Ryan Matthews wanted sexy Jessica Newman the
moment he saw her. And she seemed to want him, too, but
something was holding her back. So Ryan decides it's time
to launch a sensual assault. He *is* going to have Jessica in
his bed—and he isn't above tempting her with her own
forbidden fantasies to do it....

SIMPLY SENSUAL by Carly Phillips
January 2001

When P.I. Ben Callahan agrees to take the job of watching
over spoiled heiress Grace Montgomery, he figures it's easy
money. That is, until he discovers gorgeous Grace has a
reckless streak a mile wide and is a serious threat to his
libido—and his heart. Ben isn't worried about keeping
Grace safe. But can he protect her from his loving lies?

Don't miss this daring duo!

Visit us at www.eHarlequin.com   HTBLAZEW